I0675803

Seeing Beings is Believing Chronicles

Sing Me a Song of the Dead

Book 2

E & K. Kim

Seeing Beings is Believing Chronicles

Book 2
Sing me a song of the dead

By E. & K. Kim.
Aka The Sisters Kim
Illustrated by E & K. Kim

First published in Australia 2025
This edition published 2025
Copyright © E & K. Kim 2025

The right of E & K. Kim to be identified as the Author of the Work has been asserted in accordance with the Copyright, Designs and Patents Act 1988.

All rights reserved. No part of this publication may be reproduced, stored in a retrieval system, or transmitted, in any form or by any means without the prior written permission of the publisher, nor be otherwise circulated in any form of binding or cover other than that in which it is published and without a similar condition being imposed on the subsequent purchaser.

Disclaimer: Seeing Beings Is Believing is a work of fiction. Characters, their names, their businesses and the events and incidents involving them are the products of the author's imagination. Any resemblance to actual persons, living or dead, or actual events is purely coincidental.

E & K. Kim
Seeing Beings is Believing Chronicles - Book 2 - Sing me a song of the dead
ISBN: 978-1-7638491-6-7

About the Authors

E & K. Kim were born in Box Hill Victoria, Australia. At a young age, both sisters were interested in fantasy genres. As they got older they became even more captured by different books and movies. They started to write their own stories about beings such as vampires, wolves and creatures that are mentioned very often in popular culture.

E & K. Kim live together on a farm with their animals. They love the rural aspect that comes with living on a large property. Still being young themselves, they wanted to create a book that contained a collection of stories that aren't heard of except inside these stories that intertwine with each other.

Both sisters wish they could have read a book like this when they were younger. However, now that they get the chance to write their own stories, they hope that everyone, especially younger people never lose their creativity or the imagination they had during childhood. They both believe imagination is the key to creativity and without it the world would be a duller place. Belief in yourself and belief in something is what led E & K. Kim to come up with the Seeing Beings is Believing Chronicles.

You see what you wanna see, you do what you wanna do, you think what you wanna think.
Every story has a connection, and that is the link.

Table of Contents:

Magical Beings here and there.
Hidden Creatures everywhere.
Show your true identity.
As you are now real to me.

Map & Mythical Creature Glossary

Banshees - Country of origin: Ireland (E.g. Thomasin Dullahan)

Bunyip People - Country of origin: Australia

Succubus/Incubus - Species of demons known to fool humans. Also able to remove energy from lifeforms and magical objects/items. Country of origin: Middle East (E.g. Aisha Gregory)

Vampires - Country of origin: First Vampires originated from the Middle East (E.g. Isabella Drusillia)

Cat People - Country of origin: Egypt; also migrated to Australia and South America, see brown spots on the map, (E.g. Cleopatra Philopator)

Zomon - Zombie/Demon Hybrid created to serve demons. Place of origin: the Underworld (E.g. Groady)

Pookas - Species of waterhorse. Country of origin: Ireland

Nickurs - Species of waterhorse from Northern countries. Country of origin: All of Scandinavia

Kelpies - Species of waterhorse originally from Scotland. Country of origin: Scotland

The Ancients - Country or place of origin: Unknown

Werewolves - Country of origins: Stories based from many countries indicate that werewolves originate from and/or have no single country from where they are believed to originate. As they are popular in many cultures around the world. (E.g. Siegfried)

Witches - Country of origin: Universal mythical being. Known throughout the world and all witches are governed by the Witches Covenant.

Mute Beings (or aka as mutants. Beings that were born of a human bloodline with some or little mythical being gene. The type of mute beings with genes or which circumstances they were born from vary depending on the types of the mythical being gene they have.) (E.g. FOG and Levi Virazio)

Merwolf - Country of origin: None since they are a hybrid species. (E.g. Arianna Solaris)

Will-o-wisps - Country of origin: England (E.g. Lord Gruesome)

Headless Horseman - Creature similar to the Dullahan. Country known to be of origin: North America also known to Ireland

Ghosts - Spirits are well known around the whole world.

Fae species - (Fairies, types vary) Country of origin: No specifics

Demons - Many demons lurk in the Underworld. Origin point of demons: the Underworld (Ruler of the Hidden Empire; located in the Underworld, the Demon King)

Meerpeople - Creatures of the sea. Place believed to be origin: Atlantis/no specifics (Poseidon, King of Atlantis)

Elves - Species of beings similar to the Fae. Country of origin: Specifically based in Europe.

Dullahan - Being that runs amok at night, creating disturbances/destroying anything in its path. Country of origin: Ireland

Kitsunes - Country of origin: Japan

Hu-Hsien - Species similar to the Kitsune. Country of origin: China

Celtic Wolf - Country of origin: Germany (E.g. Fane Halfdan)

Dragons - Ancient beings worshipped around the world especially (All Asian countries, Europe)

Phoenixes - Country of origin: There are many countries that mention Phoenixes in their cultures such as (Europe, Middle East, Asia, India) (E.g. Jamari Acchamba)

Grim Reaper/Reaper associates - Country of origin: England (E.g. Thomas Reap, Lara Kraft)

Gargoyles - Statues that tend to hang around places of worship such as churches. However, they do not serve the church as one thinks. Maybe priests serve the Gargoyles. Country of origin: France (E.g. Laurent the Gargoyle)

Sing me a song of the dead

Your parents failed to raise you. Freya should never have been born, they said. You are your father's lingering shadow, they said. Freya should be dead. A good Freya is a dead Freya. They said. My mother said I will sing you a song, now it is time to sing mine.

781 AD

In the outskirts of Kattegat, a son was born to a simple farmer Ragnar and his wife Aslaug. His name was Bjorn Lothbrok.

His future name which would make him a legend was Bjorn Ironside. Bjorn in Norse means bear. In our culture, it is bad to say the word bear, which is why the name Bjorn was given to my father instead. Bjorn was an only child at first but soon to be followed by the birth of Hvitserk in 793 AD, twelve years after the birth of Bjorn. A year later Ivar was born. A child whose bones were too brittle and weak to ever assist him in walking. His name in the future was Ivar the boneless.

The least respected son of the sons of Ragnar Lothbrok. But most loved by his mother Aslaug.

In 794 AD, Sigurd was born. He had the highest temper and a selfish nature. The most hated sibling. Enemies with his older brother Ivar even though Ivar never did anything to Sigurd. Apparently, he was named after his mother's father Sigurd snake-in-the-eye. After somehow overthrowing the earl of Kattegat, Ragnar becomes king of Kattegat and so it began that Bjorn was thrown into a complex life alongside his three brothers.

Seven years later from 794 AD to 801 AD

Kattegat, the great hall: Bjorn waited patiently for his father. They

9

were to go off on a hunting trip together, being Ragnar's favourite son of course.

This year Bjorn had turned eighteen. Meanwhile, Hvitserk was six, Ivar who was pulled around on a cart on wheels by Hvitserk was five, and Sigurd the cry-baby was four. Still having heard of the potential war with the West Saxons, Ragnar still intended to leave on this hunting trip with his eldest son even though Aslaug strongly advised against it. Suddenly, Bjorn heard loud footsteps coming from the throne area. It was his father.
Ragnar grinned and hit his son on the back.

He said: 'Bjorn, it is time.'

Bjorn had his gear ready. Soon after, Ragnar took Bjorn to the ports where a friend of Ragnar's lived. A man that knew Ragnar before he became king of Kattegat.
Bjorn asked his father curiously: 'Where are you taking me?'
Ragnar laughed: 'You are very curious son.'
Ragnar said while taking long strides: 'Today, I am going to introduce you to Toki. Toki is the smartest man I know. He could even build the strongest ships that could sail to Valhalla.'
Bjorn and Ragnar arrived at the port. There was a small house on the seaside. It was a wooden den with a heaped thatched roof. Away at work was a man with an irregularly long beard and bent back. He wore the most torn and miserable clothing Bjorn had ever seen, probably because Bjorn grew up as a pampered Viking prince for most of his life.
Ragnar shook hands with the old man and said: 'Toki, have you finished the ship yet?'
Toki blinked multiple times when he said: 'No need to shout Ragnar, my ears are weakening with age.'
He muttered: 'If you are even aware of my current age.'
Toki pointed towards a ship that was at the ready, tied by the port docks. Bjorn saw the wooden ship with his own eyes. It was a black ash wood, as dark as the trees in Norway. The prow had fascinating awnings. The awning was that of a horse, a strange-looking horse.
Ragnar commended Toki: 'Good work on the Knarr ship.'
Ragnar added: 'Although the Knarr ship is only a trade ship and not for use in battle, you put so much effort into the ship, you must have gotten carried away with the build.'
Toki complained: 'You always complain about the ships I make. Can't you just be grateful that I manufactured the trade ship you ordered me to make?'
Bjorn asked the old man: 'You made that entire ship yourself, or did you have thrall help you?'
Toki frowned: 'My servants, the thrall helped me, yes.'

Ragnar followed the old man into the den. Bjorn followed after his father.

Toki asked: 'Now, now, I've met your son and you've seen the ship, what else can I do for you?'

Ragnar asked Toki: 'I was wondering whether you would like to come on a bear hunt with us?'

Toki widened his eyes and stated: 'You think me a madman?'

He continued on: 'I'm not your age, I am over fifty years old already, it's a wonder I haven't retired yet from the shipping trade.'

Ragnar: 'Alright, we might as well be on our way to the mountains.'

Toki: 'Yes and beware of the door on the way out.'

Bjorn was about to leave when he saw a peculiar woman handing Toki a cup of water.

Toki asked the woman: 'Porunn, have you chopped the wood for the fire?'

Porunn answered quickly: 'Yes master.'

Toki: 'Have you tended to the crops and goats?'

Once more she answered without hesitation: 'Yes master.'

Toki sighed heavily: 'You know Porunn, I wish you would not call me master, you may have once been a thrall, but you are now a shield maiden, there is no need to be put down like this.'

Porunn glared at Bjorn for a brief moment then crouched down to put more wood into the fire. Bjorn left with his father to go hunting.

Later: The cold freezing weather was enough to chill even the strongest of souls.

Ragnar yelled to his son: 'Bjorn, the bear went that way!'

Bjorn could feel the energy pumping through his veins. The anticipation of catching the animal lingered in his mind. Ragnar came up in front of the bear creating a distraction, meanwhile, Bjorn threw an axe at the bear from behind and then finished it off with a quick stab of a sword.

Soon after Bjorn and Ragnar returned to Kattegat.

Bjorn yelled to the villagers: 'We come bearing gifts!'

Ragnar and his family feasted on the bear meat that night. Sigurd and Ivar had a contest over who could eat the fastest, meanwhile, Hvitserk was busy trying to stop his younger brothers from fighting. Aslaug blabbered on about how she could turn some of the bear's hide into a wall covering or a bed blanket. Bjorn insisted she use some of the hide to make a cloak from it.

The next day Aslaug was handling the hide when Bjorn decided

11

to keep his mother company.

Aslaug asked: 'What's wrong? Normally you're off with Ragnar somewhere begging for adventure or trouble.'

Bjorn rolled his eyes and said: 'I think I've had enough of killing, hunting, or adventuring.'

Aslaug snickered and replied: 'That is not you, what did this Bjorn do with my son?'

Bjorn: 'Mother.'

Aslaug smiled and said: 'Son.'

Bjorn: 'Fine, I have this problem.'

Aslaug looked closer at her son and gasped. She covered her mouth with her hand after saying: 'No, it can't be!'

Bjorn asked loudly: 'What!?'

Aslaug shook her head and said: 'That is the same face your father made before he asked me to marry him.'

Bjorn: 'And?'

Aslaug: 'And you have an attraction to some woman you met, hah, I feared this day would come.'

She went on to ask: 'Now tell me, what is her name?'

Bjorn answered: 'Porunn.'

Aslaug said casually: 'I believe I've heard of her before, she's one of the new shield maidens.'

Aslaug asked: 'Why don't you go talk to her?'

Bjorn thought over it, thanked his mother for the advice, and left.

Aslaug sighed and looked at her three young sons sleeping on the bed. She said quietly: 'Which of my sons is going to fall in love next in the future?'

Bjorn saw the shield maidens fighting in the farming district of Kattegat. He looked about for Porunn but could not find her.

He asked one of the other female warriors: 'Do you know where Porunn is?'

The shield maiden pointed towards a woman shooting arrows at a haystack. She saw him approach. But kept shooting arrows.

Bjorn commentated: 'You have good aim.'

Porunn stopped and said: 'I need no lecture from a man, I will do as I please with my skills.'

Bjorn: 'Are you preparing for the war against the West Saxons?'

Porunn snapped at him: 'What a foolish question, you too should be preparing, war is nothing for children.'

Bjorn said: 'Ahem, how do I say this?'

Porunn: 'Say what?'

Bjorn: 'I like you Porunn.'

Porunn frowned and said: 'I have no time for relationships.'

Bjorn replied: 'What will it take to persuade you?'

Porunn retorted: 'Slay one enemy, they say the eldest prince of

Kattegat has good fighting skills but not close enough to slay enemies on the battlefield.'

And with that Porunn left Bjorn to wander in thought.
Ragnar and Bjorn ventured with countless warships and an army of Vikings to England to fight against the West Saxons. In the battle, Bjorn and Ragnar took down many soldiers, it was no easy feat. Porunn tried to prove that one can also fight from afar using a bow and arrows. When Porunn was focusing on shooting down an enemy, someone came from behind, she stumbled back and slashed her face on a pointy rock on the ground. Porunn held her hands to her face. Blood trickled from her wound down her neck. The assailant was about to deliver the finishing blow when Bjorn finished the attacker from behind. Bjorn pulled his sword out of the man and the man fell to the ground. Porunn was ashamed to let anyone see her face. Bjorn pulled up Porunn and let her lean on him for support.
After the victory against the West Saxons, the Vikings retreated to their homes, returning to Kattegat in Norway. Bjorn saw to it that Porunn was taken care of under the roof of his family. Toki would occasionally visit Porunn to see how she was fairing. Porunn was disgusted with herself and wanted no one's pity. Every day she would say to the healers how she dreaded living. Her face was no longer hers and she was scarred for life, be it emotionally or physically. It took many months for Porunn to recover. Bjorn waited till he got the chance to talk to her. Aslaug kept trying to understand what he saw in the woman.

Time passed and one day Porunn was ready to leave. Bjorn tried everything to persuade her to stay. He even reminded her that she said that if he slew one or more enemies, she would be convinced of his feelings for her. Porunn was left speechless when he asked her to take a leap of faith with him and start a relationship with him.

At the beginning of the new year 802 AD:
Porunn was in a strong and intimate relationship with Bjorn. Aslaug would always judge Porunn since Porunn used to be a thrall (servant), especially when Bjorn had Porunn join him at dinner with his family. Aslaug stared intensely at Porunn over the dinner table. Ragnar sat in between Ivar and Sigurd to prevent them from fighting. But the two youngsters let their vengeance out on someone else. Hvitserk sat on his mother's lap. Ivar and Sigurd threw food at their father. Porunn sat there next to Bjorn, a face as pale as a white bedsheet. Aslaug could not stand the eerie silence any longer. She drank a mouthful of mead from her cup that was made from an animal's horns. Porunn's stomach began to grumble loudly - very LOUDLY.
Ragnar laughed and stated to Porunn's embarrassing body: 'Your

stomach sounds like the ocean is waging war.'
Porunn gaped at Ragnar when she could not take it in any longer:
The annoying children, Ragnar's ridiculous remark, Aslaug's scorching
stare, Bjorn's concerned face.
Porunn blurted out rather loudly: 'I'm with child.'
Bjorn's eyes widened so much that they looked like they were going
to slide right out of their sockets.
Ragnar said: 'Whaaaaat?'
And told Ivar and Sigurd to shut up. Aslaug choked on her drink
and spewed out what she drank. Poor Hvitserk was gonna need a
clean-up from his mummy-mouth-mead-spill disaster. Hvitserk began to
cry and ran away from Aslaug.
Aslaug asked, still in shock: 'Wh-what?'
Ragnar: 'You didn't mean what you said right? Right?'
Bjorn calmed down and said to his parents: 'Stop it, so what, the
two of you are going to be grandparents.'
Ragnar: 'Yes but isn't it a bit early, I mean your child could be the
sibling of your younger brothers and they don't understand that they
are the child's uncle!'
Aslaug: 'And you aren't even married, not that it matters to Vikings
but it matters to me, I want to see my son happily married.'
Bjorn sighed miserably and said: 'Fine, me and Porunn will wed.'
Porunn asked quickly: 'Are you sure?'
Bjorn: 'Yes or my mother will never stop bugging us.'

A week later, 802 AD
Porunn got dressed. A special event was being held in Kattegat.
Everyone was excited about the wedding of the eldest son of king
Lothbrok. On that day, Aslaug gifted her son a cloak she had made from
the bear hide to wear to his wedding. Toki gave the woman whom he
cared for as his own daughter his blessing to wed.

And so it became that Porunn was now part of the Lothbrok family.
Nine months later: Porunn had come to a full term in her pregnancy
and had begun labour. Bjorn sat outside the room listening in on his
wife who was screeching out in agony. Aslaug paced the room back
and forth in waiting. This continued on for another two hours.
Toki was told by a woman that was helping deliver the child: 'There
are certain complications, the child still has not come yet.'
Toki was infuriated. Clearly worried about Porunn more than
Lothbroks, he rattled the thrall:
'What sort of complications!' Toki demanded to know.
Bjorn playing the hero got up and said: 'I know what to do, if it
may help though, I do not know.'
Aslaug: 'Are you going to pray to Odin again at the Odense?'

14

Bjorn nodded and wandered off.

Aslaug mumbled: 'Even though Odin is associated with war.'

Bjorn kneeled in front of the stone slab and statue of Odin.

He said: 'Please help Porunn bring our son into this world, I want nothing more than to meet my son.'

Then he became earnest and said: 'Oh great Odin, wise ancestor of Lothbrok, I beg upon you for your help, I'm sorry that I expect you to do something that is not of your interest, being a god that is associated with war, but I worship you and trust you, Odin ... in this time of need for our son, I did not know what god to turn to.'

Meanwhile, Porunn was still in the living hell. She strained herself now, and suddenly a baby started to cry. Porunn looked at the woman who was cradling the infant and smiled. Daughter or son, it did not matter as long as Bjorn and her could be one happy family. After the thrall had cleaned her baby, they gave the child to her to hold. Porunn looked at her child, her daughter. Then she saw something strange on her daughter's face. She saw damaged skin.

Porunn yelled out: 'Get that hideous thing away from me! Get it away!'

The thrall put the child away from sight for now.

Bjorn came storming into the room since he heard his wife's commotion. Porunn was so stressed out that she struggled to breathe for air. She could not believe that she had given birth to something so - UGLY. Porunn held her hands to her face, she felt the huge scar on her face. She started to tremble, sitting upright on the bed.

She screeched: 'I-I can't do this anymore! First my face now my child!'

Bjorn told the thrall to bring in the child. He was in the other room now with Aslaug. A thrall passed him the child. He rejoiced at first then crept back when he saw the child's face.

He managed to ignore what he considered a BIRTH DEFECT and asked a thrall (servant/slave): 'Is it a boy or girl?'

The slave replied: 'A girl.'

The words 'a girl' echoed in his mind. He shoved the baby back into the care of that thrall and stormed off in disappointment and rage. It was after all a son he wanted and not a daughter. Porunn tried to talk to him later on, but he completely ignored his wife. Feeling so useless she put on her gear and left on a raid the next day with a group of Vikings, no matter her drained condition after childbirth, she did not care. That recklessness was enough to get her killed. Soon after, the ship returned to Kattegat, the raid unsuccessful. Porunn deceased. One of the Viking men went to the great hall to report to King Lothbrok that the wife of his eldest son had died.

Ragnar knew immediately that the woman would not be missed by his son. He knew Bjorn would be the type to easily take woman after

woman and not care. Ragnar sat on his throne and asked himself:
'What has become of the honourable house of Lothbrok?'
In the meantime, Aslaug was cradling her granddaughter and said:
'No, you aren't bad, it's not your fault that you are the way you are.'

Aslaug looked at the baby's weakened skin on its face.
Aslaug said: 'When you grow up, I'm sure that skin will go right
away, you'll grow out of it, I promise.'
Hvitserk ran up to his mother. He said: 'Mummy, Sigurd is pulling
Ivar about.'
Aslaug laughed her loud, long laugh and said: 'You really love
taking care of Ivar.'
Hvitserk said: 'Ivar needs help, Sigurd's being a bully.'
Aslaug stated to the six-year-old: 'Ivar isn't so weak as you think
Hvitserk, he has more will and strength than all your brothers combined
... Ivar will be alright.'
Hvitserk said: 'But he can't walk.'
Aslaug: 'There are many forms of strengths that are not to be
underestimated.'
Hvitserk asked: 'Who is this?'
He looked at the baby that his mother was holding.

Aslaug replied: 'She is Bjorn's daughter, and she too has a lot of
willpower ... too much for her own good.'

816 AD
Bjorn was the king of Kattegat now at the age of thirty-two. This was
fourteen years later after his daughter had been born in 802 AD. The
girl whose very existence he resented. Bjorn was king due to the fact
that Ragnar had mysteriously disappeared in 814 AD. Aslaug had
withdrawn from ruling duties as queen since that job was now her
son's. She had also raised all her sons to full age. Hvitserk was twenty
years old. Ivar was nineteen years old, and Sigurd was eighteen years
old. The girl that lived under the same roof was currently being raised
by her grandmother Aslaug. Aslaug was always a sort of parent role for
her. The name that her father had given her was Asa. Bjorn had in this
time gained the epithet name 'Ironside' from his people, and well the
citizens of Kattegat ridiculed Ivar and his leg contraptions. They gave
him the epithet: 'Ivar the boneless'. Asa was so hated by her father that
she was forbidden to be even within his near radius or to be seen by his
eyes. Aslaug was hanging out cloaks to dry when Asa came out to help.
Aslaug asked: 'Dear child, what brings you out here?'
Asa pried: 'Grandmother, I want to know the truth about my
mother.'
Aslaug said in a casual tone: 'There is nothing to be said.'
Asa: 'You and I both know you are lying.'

Aslaug shook her head and kept on working.
Asa tried again: 'My mother, Porunn, what happened to her? Grandmother?'
Aslaug: 'Where on earth did you hear that name?'
Asa: 'Does it matter?'
Aslaug grabbed the girl's hands and squeezed them.

She replied: 'If your father hears you talk about these things, he'll send you away for good, away from the last people that care about you.'
Asa lowered her face: 'My mother did abandon me but is dead, she died, I just want to know why she left me alone.'
Aslaug touched the girl's face where the weak skin used to be.
She said: 'Granddaughter, you are not alone. You have me and your uncles ... doesn't Hvitserk teach you Norse and Ivar teach you to fight?'
Aslaug said: 'Sigurd's useless, that I know but the other two care about you.'
Asa: 'I suppose you're right, I'm sorry, I don't know what came over me and I hate myself for still wanting to know more about the people that isolated me and for wanting to best father.' Asa went on to say: 'I hate his guts, I wish he'd just ...'
Aslaug cut her off and said: 'You'd do best not to finish that sentence.'
Asa went about. A bored teen. Sigurd was off gambling with his money.
Asa told him: 'You know Uncle, your mother hates your irresponsible nature and your garlic breath. I can smell it without having to sit across from you.'
Sigurd complained: 'Mother does not care since she's always too busy worrying about Ivar.'
Sigurd was so drunk that he attempted to impersonate his mother: 'Oooooh, I need to go find Mister Boneless, oh no, Bjorn is going to send off my poor Ivar to a raid.'
Asa stood there. A frown as strong as iron.
The other man who had been gambling with her uncle sniffed the stench from Sigurd and said: 'Ew you stink. I stink Viking but you stink dead.'
The man left the money to Sigurd and hurried off.
Sigurd pointed at the fair amount of money and said: 'See, it pays to stink like hell and get the man's money without having to gamble at all.'
Asa rolled her eyes and left.

She went to visit Toki. The ship master. Apparently, he had been a close friend of her grandfather and a fatherly role to her mother Porunn. Toki sat in his den. Asa knocked on the open door. Toki saw Asa duck her head in through the door. He motioned her to come in. He warmed himself over the fire.
Asa said: 'I see you are always freezing here in this part of Kattegat.'

She shivered and asked the old man: 'So, do you want to continue telling me the story of Thor and his great battle against the eternal serpent Jorgmungandr?'

Toki laughed and said: 'Ah Asa, you remind me so much of your mother, that was also her most favourite story.'

Toki became a bit sad.

He said: 'I-I shouldn't be talking about your mother. I just miss Porunn so much. Even if she did abandon you. I am forbidden to tell or say any more than that in the presence of Bjorn's daughter.'

Asa snapped at him: 'Who forbids such nonsense?'

Toki stuttered: 'Y-your f-father.'

Asa scowled: 'Why is everything and everyone a lie!'

She said: 'I just wish I met one kind soul other than my two uncles. Someone who makes me feel like I exist.'

She stormed off.

Toki: 'That side is from her father though.'

The next day, Aslaug looked about for Asa. Asa was off cutting wood. It was something she enjoyed doing. Aslaug was wanting to speak to Ivar and Hvitserk about Asa. Ivar was talking to Hvitserk about how much Bjorn had changed in the last fourteen years when their mother walked up to them. Ivar could not walk. He leaned against the wall. The strappy contraptions to keep his legs straight. Ivar had the personality of fire. Strong but a struggling flickering flame underestimated by everybody. Deep within though was a caring personality, a warm person. One must look beyond the title 'boneless' and beyond the temper to see that truth. Hvitserk had the personality of water. He was calm and subtle like peaceful fleeting water. However, when provoked in the wrong way, the water would flood and drown all sources of hope and light. Sigurd had the personality of wind, crazy loud, blowing everything away, mostly in a bad way.

Aslaug asked Ivar: 'How are you fairing?'

Ivar answered charmingly: 'I'm doing fine.'

Aslaug asked Hvitserk: 'And you, how are you fairing as Bjorn's advisor?'

Hvitserk answered: 'It's been hard work mother but it's working.'

Aslaug became serious: 'There is something I'd like the two of you to do for me.'

Ivar asked: 'What's eating you mother?'

Aslaug shoved him and said: 'Stop talking like that, lest people think you are also a barbarian.'

Ivar: 'I am only embracing the truth mother, Vikings are barbarians.'

Aslaug said: 'Anyway, ignoring Ivar's strange remark, I'd like the two of you to enrol Asa as a shield maiden.'

Ivar laughed: 'Yes, I bet Asa would be a great shield maiden. Especially with those clean cuts she makes when she chops wood. Imagine the–'
Aslaug stopped him and said: 'I understand Ivar, no need to go into detail. I think building her out as a shield maiden would give her more distance between her and her father as well as take her mind off things.'
Ivar asked: 'What sort of things?'
Aslaug: 'She has been telling me she has trouble sleeping at night. She dreams of killing her father. She dreams of a vast field of dead people.'
Hvitserk: 'Then maybe she shouldn't become a shield maiden, considering dead people and blood-stained fields are amongst some of the many things she will see as a shield maiden.'
Aslaug said: 'No, sometimes we must face our fears, no matter how daunting things may seem, and even the most dreadful of experiences can help us overcome our darkest of things.'
Aslaug: 'Besides, Asa also tells me that as every day passes, she feels less and less alive. As if the world put her there and no longer acknowledges her.'

A few days later: Aslaug told Asa that she was soon to begin training as a shield maiden. Aslaug saw that Asa showed no reaction whatsoever.
She also went to go tell her eldest son Bjorn of her decision. Bjorn sat on the wooden throne. The same throne Ragnar sat on and those rulers that came before him. Aslaug saw the plain expression on her son's face.
He said loudly: 'What could be so important to drag my mother here?'
Aslaug: 'Your daughter starts training tomorrow as a shield maiden.'
Bjorn sneered: 'And I could not care less. Do with her as you please as long as she stays out of my sight.'
As the sun rose, Aslaug nagged Asa to get dressed in her gear and get out of bed. Asa, who continuously rubbed her eyes to wake up, went with Hvitserk to the training of the shield maidens. She and her uncle were in a district of Kattegat she had never even seen before but only heard about. The class of Karl, the farmers tending to the fields that were with an abundance of crops. Though the workers looked quite strained, so much hard work for all those crops.
Hvitserk left his niece with the shield maidens. The shield maidens laughed at Asa as she introduced herself. One of the nasty warrior women laughed and spat on the floor in front of Asa.
She said: 'Sounds like Ass. Welcome Ass to the shield maidens training group. Let's just hope you are strong. You don't even have to

have too many brains, as long as you don't hit yourself with your own weapon. Ingrid did that and lost a foot. She's a peg-leg now.' Ingrid waved to Asa and showed her proud peg-leg.

Asa looked down in horror at the wooden peg-leg.

The nasty one went on to say: 'In this line of work you can't afford to be afraid or lazy. So, as long as Miss Asa doesn't sit on her ass, she'll be fine.'

Asa said: 'Neither should shield maidens be so cocky.'

The nasty one was infuriated and punched Asa in the face. Asa landed on one knee.

Shield maiden said: 'Wow, I got the daughter of the king on one knee, she's kneeling to me!'

The others laughed. Ingrid placed a weapon on Asa and said: 'Don't make the same mistake I did, or you'll end up losing a thing or two or three.'

Asa gripped the axe handle tightly and had this lingering hatred in her mind. The problem with Asa is when someone pisses her off, she's eternally pissed off. Asa is super stubborn and has her immense twisted pride so it's a real turn-off when someone says she can't do this or that. To add to that, she had her father's emotional temper drive. At that moment she wanted to prove to those shield maidens that she wasn't just a heap of uselessness. Just like she wanted nothing more than to prove to her father that she existed which was why she picked up combat lessons with Ivar in the first place. She even learned to read and write the most difficult Norse texts with Hvitserk. But that wasn't good enough either! She hated her father and yet ... She went to all that trouble to try and sway her father, to convince him she existed. Why?! She yelled: 'Why! Why am I not good enough! Lies! Lies. I-I hate myself.'

She took that axe and began chopping like a mad man at a wooden post.

Ingrid said: 'Save your breath, you won't manage to chop that down in one day.'

Asa yelled: 'I don't care! I am not good enough. So, I'll find a way to be good enough!'

The shield maidens let Asa have her way. Asa swung that axe up and down for hours on end till night. Not thinking. Not caring anymore. She let go, of everything. Her hatred. Her pride. Her selfishness. And looked the truth in the eye: she was an idiot. She had been raised as an idiot. But that would always stay. So, she used her new will to swing the axe one more time and then the wood splintered and broke into many pieces. The shield maidens looked at her in disbelief. The nasty shield maiden chuckled and said: 'You're a crazy one, but I'll give you this, you're gonna be one heck of a shield maiden.'

The head maiden passed Asa a silver arm ring.
She said: 'You're officially one of us. Keep the axe, you're pretty good with it.'

That day Asa was the same person, but a new will was completely reinforced. From now on she refused to be put down by her father. She would not strive to prove her existence but strive to prove she was worth more than him. But that would be something she would decide when and where. She would do things on her account now. She went home for once, deciding that the world could not prove that she existed. This was something that she must do. For once she had her head held high. As Asa trod in through the door, Aslaug saw the strange, determined look on her granddaughter's face.

Aslaug smiled and said to herself: 'So making her become a shield maiden was the trick.'
She saw the gleaming arm ring Asa held. She was proud that her grandchild achieved so much in her life.
Later: Aslaug was visiting Bjorn. He had this tired expression on his face.
Aslaug asked Bjorn: 'Don't you need a break son?'
Bjorn yawned and said: 'No.'
Aslaug laughed and said: 'I wonder what I could do for you that would lift your spirits.'
Bjorn said casually: 'Nothing.'
Aslaug smiled and said: 'Sure?'
Aslaug groaned: 'This is suffering. Son, you are causing all of us to suffer. Do you know how many debts you have to pay? How many judgements you must still pass in Kattegat?'
Bjorn said: 'Yes, yes.'
Aslaug suggested: 'How about you re-marry?'
Bjorn shook his head and said: 'No comment.'
Aslaug: 'Listen, if you don't care, there is a nice shield maiden woman down at outer Kattegat. Her name is Ingrid, and she has a magnificent club foot.'
Bjorn yelled: 'Look mother, I'm not interested!'
Aslaug grinned and replied: 'I'll find a way then to make you interested, because even if you have no heir other than Asa, you hate the poor girl so much you'd never let her take your place.'
Bjorn said defiantly: 'Over my dead body! I'd rather let Hvitserk take over.'
Aslaug left and said in her mind: 'Poor Hvitserk, isn't it bad enough already that he's your advisor?'
For the next months, Aslaug searched far and wide in Kattegat for a woman that was special enough for Bjorn. Strangely a woman

wrote a letter of a plea for help to Aslaug.
It said:

Dearest friend, I know you do not remember me. I know that you were friends with my mother when you were both girls. But after you married you stayed in Kattegat and my mother left for Denmark. I am the daughter of a woman you once loved as a friend. It is my greatest sorrow to say that she has died.

My name is Elleswith and am in urgent need of help. A strange entity has been chasing me in Denmark for a lengthy period of time. I assure you, I will do anything in return if you help me get into Kattegat. I am not able to walk in the open with a stalker around the corner. Burn this letter once you have read this. If you shall help me, I will be very grateful.

Elleswith.

Soon after, Aslaug rushed to help this Elleswith since this young woman was the daughter of a friend that had been very dear to her.
Aslaug managed to get Elleswith into Kattegat without being seen. Elleswith seemed to be a tall woman. A young woman probably nineteen to twenty years old.
With her was a man who looked over Elleswith with great care.

His name was Hastein. Elleswith wore a cloak to conceal herself. Aslaug brought Elleswith to her home that was near the great hall.

That was the same place in which her granddaughter Asa lived as well. Aslaug could only pray that none of her other sons would be visiting here the next few days. Aslaug motioned Elleswith to sit down at a chair near the fire. Aslaug was preparing a place for Elleswith to sleep.

Hastein took the cloak from Elleswith. Aslaug turned around to tell Elleswith the house rules when she saw the most beautiful woman she had ever seen sit before her. Elleswith's eyes sparkled.
She said: 'That's the same face everyone gives me. Hence the use of the cloak.'

Elleswith had long chestnut coloured, messy locks of hair falling to her waist. She had the most slender body and mesmerising eyes.
Aslaug blurted out: 'Refrain from going out too much and from waking up Asa who sleeps in the next room across from you.'
Aslaug asked her: 'Who is this man, this Hastein, to you?'
Elleswith looked up at the aged man and said: 'He's my foster father. He was my mother's thrall but after she died, he stayed to look after me. We've been family ever since.'
Aslaug said before she herself went to sleep: 'Very well, in that aspect, he may stay.'

The next morning Asa awoke to help her grandmother with chores when she found a stranger lying on a makeshift bed.
Asa stammered: 'H-hey w-who a-are you?'
Asa stepped back a bit. Elleswith woke up and stretched.
She said to Asa: 'Ah you must be this Asa that Aslaug told me about.' Elleswith smiled.
Asa said in an annoyed voice: 'That still doesn't explain who you are or what you are doing here!'
Elleswith laughed.
She said: 'Here, it's as simple as this, give me your hand.'
Asa had a puzzled look on her face. Strangely she was compelled to give the woman her hand. Elleswith shook hands with Asa.
She said: 'It's nice to meet you, my name is Elleswith.'
Asa frowned: 'Eh, nice to meet you Elleswith.'
But in her mind, she asked herself: How can a mere stranger bond with me so fast in comparison with my grandmother who raised me, with whom I am yet to establish a stronger connection?
Elleswith stood up and dusted off her garment using her hands.
Elleswith said to Asa: 'You know, the name Asa does not suit you all too well.'
Asa said: 'You act like you know me so well.'
Elleswith said: 'But no, it would be lovely to get to know you. As for your face, I can sense a brutally strong-willed person with a very twisted, complex nature. But even you have a problem. Deep within you, there is a voice yet to be freed. The chains are starting to break but the brand of one's soul still binds you to one place.'
Elleswith put a hand on Asa's shoulder and said: 'You seem to be unhappy. I can see it in your eyes and hear it in your voice.'

23

Asa growled: 'You're insane.' She wacked off Elleswith's hand and ran outside.

Asa refused to let a stranger understand her. Asa ran right into Hastein. The tall masculine man knocked over Asa. Even though in Asa's training she learned to hold her stance no matter what the situation, Asa toppled right over. And hit her head. She was unconscious. Hastein carried the girl back inside. Elleswith saw Asa being held by Hastein. Hastein put Asa down on the bed. Elleswith ran her hand over Asa's forehead. There was a bruise.

Elleswith asked Hastein: 'Is there anyone around?'

Hastein shook his head. Elleswith rolled up her sleeve and covered the bruise with the palm of her hand. Elleswith closed her eyes and concentrated hard.

Asa opened her eyes and asked Elleswith: 'I am a fool or not?'

Elleswith said with closed eyes: 'Perhaps, but being a fool does not make you a bad person.'

Asa felt the bruise being healed on her forehead. For once, Asa felt that someone truly cared about her. Even if it was someone with strange abilities.

Asa said: 'Thank you.'

Elleswith said while removing her hand from Asa's forehead: 'It seems you're not afraid of me and what I can do ...' Elleswith's voice trailed off.

Asa smiled for the first time and said: 'Perhaps if everyone had your concept of kindness, we'd have fewer fools like me and my father in this world.'

Elleswith: 'You are no fool. You need to be free, that is all.'

Asa looked up at the bare ceiling and said: 'Free ... Freya. That is the name that means free in Norse.'

Elleswith: 'Freya Lothbrok, sounds good. Freya suits you.'

Asa left the house that day. She looked at the sky and saw the birds fly. Asa raised her hand to the sky and smiled slightly. From that day forward, every day she would be known as Freya. The following days she visited Elleswith. She grew close to the woman. So close that Freya began to consider her family.

One day Freya was informed by the shield maidens they would be fighting yet another battle in England. In a place called Mercia. Freya steeled herself and said her goodbyes to Elleswith. Meanwhile, Elleswith was stitching Hasteins's shirt.

She said: 'You know foster father, you ought to be more careful out there.'

Suddenly she accidentally stitched too fast and pricked herself with her own needle. Elleswith wiped the drop of blood from her finger and remembered something from the past. A burning town. A past forgotten. A flag fading away from the fire engulfing it. Elleswith shook her head to clear her mind. That was a memory from her past as a child. Something she wished to forget but couldn't.

A voice rasped in her mind: 'You cannot escape. You will never get away! Never!'

Elleswith screeched out: 'Stop!'

That's when Freya entered the room.

She asked Elleswith: 'Are you alright?'

Elleswith said while sitting herself up properly: 'Y-yes yes, I'm fine.' She smiled nervously.

Freya asked again: 'Are you sure?'

Elleswith said: 'No not really that okay.'

Elleswith said: 'But I'll tell you this another time when you are ready to know the truth.'

Freya told Elleswith that she was heading to a battle in Mercia, England.

Elleswith said: 'It's your first battle as a shield maiden, congratulations.'

Freya smiled and said: 'Goodbye. For now.'

Freya went out the door. Motivated by her friend's kind words she went forth on a battleship just like those Vikings did before her. On the way there, she imagined Ivar complaining about his leg contraptions, Hvitserk reading a parchment in the shade and Aslaug would turn to smile at her. She felt her spirits lift. A hope that gave her something to look forward to. Freya did not enjoy fighting. She enjoyed doing something where she felt included. Even if it meant getting herself killed, she rejoiced in the fact that it was a decision she made for herself. As did all Vikings. On the battlefield, she fought. Helping the Vikings to gain yet another victory. 'Sticks and stones cannot break my bones. My heart bleeds. I feel sad and yet know I always have all of you at my side, making this weapon I wield lighter. I know I will have blood on my hands the time after I return. I must fight in order to live over my father's reputation. That is the reason, even if I want to deny it. I will tear the curtain and bring in the light you all give me. And with this light, I will live every day happily as my last!' This Freya said to herself as she fought so vigorously.

Meanwhile, in Kattegat: Elleswith was curled up in bed. A body not trembling from the cold but from the fear.

A voice screamed: 'No! Take me back! We have to save Mother and Father!'

Another voice boomed: 'We have to go Elleswith, it's too late!'

The girl was being pulled by Hastein's strong grip.

Elleswith who was young, saw the flag burning in the distance. The flag that signified the noble family where Elleswith lived and was born into. The house of Yanmir. Elleswith screamed. She woke up now. She saw Aslaug stand before her.

Aslaug said to Elleswith: 'I have a proposal for you.'

Elleswith asked while becoming more awake: 'What can I do for you?'

Aslaug said with a hint of hesitation: 'Will you marry my son? Be at his side? He needs someone he can trust. Someone he can rely on.'

Elleswith stared at Aslaug and said: 'I don't know what to say to this.'

Aslaug: 'Please. Ever since the incident with Porunn, he's been so broken. You are a beautiful woman and I believe that with your charms you could easily win him over. Besides you promised me you'd repay your debt to me.'

Elleswith's eyes widened.

She asked Aslaug: 'Who is Porunn?'

Aslaug: 'Freya's mother.'

Elleswith remembered how close she had become to Freya. The only true friend she ever had. And now she was forced to push her away and put a man first.

Elleswith asked: 'Do I have a choice in the matter?'

Aslaug was saddened.

She answered: 'No. I've already discussed this with Hastein. He said it would be best for you to stay in Kattegat. And I can't hide you in here forever. Under Bjorn's protection, you would be safe. But only through marriage.'

Elleswith answered in a casual, emotionless tone: 'Very well, I will do as you bid of me. As long as Freya is okay with this. Otherwise, I will never forgive you. Freya means more to me than you can ever comprehend.'

Elleswith was right. Aslaug could indeed not comprehend the level of the bond Elleswith shared with Freya.

The next day: Aslaug took Elleswith to meet Bjorn. Bjorn seemed to be occupied today. Aslaug told Elleswith to wait in the great hall entrance. Aslaug left for a brief moment. After a few minutes, Elleswith jumped a bit at the sound of scraping on the floor. Out of a doorway, on the opposite side of the great hall, there came two young men. Elleswith looked curiously at the man who leaned against the wall. She had heard from Freya that she had an uncle named Ivar. He wore strappy leg contraptions to help keep his legs straight since he was born without bones in his legs. Ivar looked up at the woman standing in the far corner who was looking at him. They were looking at each other as if they had never seen the sort of people exist before.

Hvitserk turned to Ivar and said: 'As I said before, both axes and swords have their uses, but wooden shields can be useful as well. You can hit enemies over the head with them and shield oneself from–' Hvitserk noticed his brother wasn't listening to him and saw what had caught Ivar's attention.

Hvitserk asked her: 'May we help you?'

He said: 'My name is Hvitserk, the one next to me, my brother's name is Ivar.'

Elleswith answered still lost in thought: 'My name is Elleswith.'

Elleswith snapped out of it and replied: 'No, I am alright.'

Hvitserk: 'Are you seeking to speak to our older brother Bjorn?'

Elleswith replied: 'I suppose so.'

Ivar joked to Hvitserk: 'Got a soft spot for women, heh?'

Hvitserk complained to Ivar: 'I have no such thing brother.'

Ivar: 'So, Hvitserk, what was this you were saying about wooden shields?'

Hvitserk said sarcastically: 'Aha, you were listening!' Ivar wanted to say something when Bjorn came and sat on his throne. Aslaug stood next to the throne and motioned for Elleswith to come closer. Bjorn looked at her.

He asked his mother: 'Who is this?'

Aslaug: 'I told you I would find a woman for you to marry. Her name is Elleswith, she is from Denmark.'

Bjorn said to Elleswith: 'Are you aware that I am thirty-two and you are only nineteen or twenty years of age?'

Elleswith nodded but said nothing. To Ivar and Hvitserk it became obvious that Elleswith had no interest nor feelings for Bjorn. It was an arranged marriage by Aslaug. Aslaug though was blinded by the thought that she was doing the best for Bjorn. Ivar though felt intrigued by Elleswith. She was the first woman that didn't look at him in disgust. She had been kind and polite. He couldn't believe that a woman like her was going to marry his older brother. Freya returned soon after. Being proud after having completed her first mission, she was excited to see the people again. The people who had enabled her to tear the curtain of her inner being and let in the light. She went past the great hall to hear the commotion.

She tried to hear what was going on: 'Skol to the marriage of Bjorn Ironside and Elleswith.'

Freya stepped back at first then she felt the devastation run amok in her heart.

She remembered the phrase she had from her mind on the battlefield: 'My heart is bleeding.'

Freya ran off. She shouted from the top of her lungs so that all of Kattegat could hear her: 'Hearts don't bleed, they yearn. Mine bleeds though!'

817 AD:

One year later, Elleswith was married to Bjorn Ironside. She was one of the Lothbroks now. She did well in helping Bjorn rule over Kattegat. Hvitserk went off and gladly called Elleswith 'Sister'.

Meanwhile, Ivar felt wrong doing so and addressed her as Elleswith instead. Bjorn kept his distance from his wife except for various occasions.

Elleswith though never got the kindness repaid that she gave to all. Freya, the only one who ever seemed to care, had kept her distance this whole year. And whenever Elleswith saw a chance to talk or even approach Freya, Freya would storm off. Freya was in a stable one day head buried in her lap, sitting on the ground. When Ivar came and sat down on a tree stump, he said to her: 'Didn't expect you here. Hoped I would find a spot to clear my head.'

Freya raised her head and said: 'So, Uncle, it seems you've been having problems lately.'

Ivar: 'It seems that the first woman to ever accept me for who I am, was meant to be with someone else.'

Freya said to him: 'It sounds weird when you say it like that, Uncle.'

Ivar chuckled and said: 'And it's funny when someone as careless and stubborn as you finds the time to reproach me on something like this.'

Freya scoffed: 'Hah, what do we do now?'

Ivar: 'I've come to a decision.'

Freya: 'What do you mean?'

Ivar: 'I know I have feelings for Elleswith. I'm not sure if it is what people call love, but I care about her. She tries to understand me. Her smile is enough to subside even the greatest of pain in this world. I would give anything to walk a path with her, to be there to hold her hand just once.'

Freya wanted to cry. Instead, she laughed.

Ivar retorted: 'Hey, what's so funny?!'

Freya acted out: 'You've been helpful, Uncle, I know now myself what I am to do. I know that Elleswith isn't happy with Bjorn. And that the marriage was arranged, she didn't have much of a choice. The facts don't change, Elleswith is still my best friend.'

A day later: Freya decided to talk to Elleswith. Elleswith stood there in her room in the great hall when she saw Freya stand in the doorway. Elleswith dropped what she was holding and said in a surprised tone: 'Freya!'

Freya sat down with Elleswith.

They talked like old friends would for a while till Elleswith became serious and said: 'Freya, I promised you I would tell you about the thing you asked about before you left for the battle of Mercia.'

Elleswith stated firmly: 'Though what I'm about to tell you, you must tell no one else. Not a soul, the only person who knows is Hastein since he's been with me for most of my life. Freya, you know I have strange abilities, right? And there's a reason why I have my long hair so it covers my ears.'

Elleswith pulled back strands of her smooth hair. Freya gasped.

She saw pointed ears. Like those creatures in the stories Hvitserk had told her and Ivar from old scrolls. Creatures that are called elves. Freya asked: 'So, you are an elf?'

Elleswith: 'Yes, I am an elf, a pureblood, one of the last.'

Freya: 'But why? Why are you one of the last pureblood elves?'

Elleswith grew solemn: 'We exist in other species called fairies and have mixed in with humans over time, while the original bloodlines were chased or hunted to the brink of extinction. I am one of the last descendants of the ancients. The ancients were once the highest of Fae kind, watching over us in the skies above, till they fell and scattered across various continents of the earth. We evolved into many different fae species. The elven kind being the last to retain the most magic and original form. The allmother of the elven kind grew to hate the species. That is how we fell. Our polar opposite species, the demons, some of them began to resent the elven kind as well. They are one of the reasons my kind is nearly extinct.'

Freya said: 'Grandmother told me you came here because you were being stalked by an unknown entity. Were they perhaps a demon?'

Elleswith: 'Yes, a dark evil vampire. All I know is he is responsible for the death of the Yanmir clan.'

Freya asked clearly interested: 'Yanmir, that is the name of a noble Danish family.'

Elleswith opened up the scroll she held. It was a family tree. It said, 'House of Yanmir.' Freya saw all the names of ancestors and descendants. At the bottom somewhere was Elleswith's name.

Freya asked: 'How old is this scroll? This long scroll.'

Elleswith answered: 'Very old, dates back to the founders of the house of Yanmir who were from Iceland, they went to Denmark and started the Yanmir bloodline.'

Above the name Elleswith, were the names of her mother and father. Freya saw a name she had heard before, 'Olenna.'

Freya mumbled: 'How strange.'

Elleswith asked: 'What?'

Freya said: 'Grandmother fondly spoke of a childhood friend named Olenna.'

Elleswith explained: 'Yes, my mother was friends with your grandmother and ... the sister of Ragnar Lothbrok.'

Freya gasped: 'What!' Elleswith told Freya to hush.

Elleswith explained: 'My mother told me this many times, Ragnar was a child born to a family in the rank of Karl in outer Kattegat. His mother though had an affair with a pureblood elf. He was later killed by Ragnar's father. Ragnar grew up with his half-sister Olenna who had been born as a result of that affair. Olenna though was a half-breed. Ragnar had to raise his half-sibling in secrecy out of fear that his father would discover the child. Aslaug, being a child in the village, befriended Olenna and that is how Aslaug met Ragnar, her future husband. Hastein

29

who had served the Karl family of Lothbrok for multiple years before Ragnar had been born was now the thrall of Ragnar. Ragnar knew well that over the years as his sister grew up that he could not hide her forever so when she was a teen, Ragnar told Hastein to take his sister and flee to another Viking country of his choosing. Olenna and Hastein disappeared together to Denmark. Ragnar never saw his sister again. Olenna and Hastein eventually found a place where there was elven kind. They were only a small handful of pureblood elves and were called the house of Yanmir.

Soon after Olenna was grown up, being half-elven she was invited to be part of Yanmir. She married into the noble family and had a daughter named Elleswith. Hastein continued to serve Olenna. Though, one night a tragedy took place. An unknown enemy burned the home of Yanmir to the ground, leaving no one left from the family or bloodline. No one but me. Which is why I've been on the run for most of my life. This vampire will stop at nothing to kill what is left of my family.'

Freya said in a concerned manner: 'Nothing will happen to you. You have me and Ivar, Hvitserk, as well as grandmother.'

Elleswith: 'I wish I had your strength, Freya.'

Freya leaned on Elleswith's shoulder. She closed her eyes, wishing to doze off.

Freya said quietly: 'I need you to see in this world.'

Elleswith had tears rolling down her cheeks.

She said to Freya: 'Do you want me to sing you a song? It's a song my mother and father sang to me.'

Freya was asleep. Elleswith began to sing the tune: 'As all stars fall, many dozen big and small. A hope that had been born, now forlorn. Light scatters across the vast veil, piercing the heart of the belief that good would always prevail. In the white light, with eyes open wide, awaken and embrace the new days before it is lost again in thy ways.' Elleswith continued to sing.

Meanwhile, Ivar stood outside of the room listening in to the beautiful voice. Ivar wanted to be with her, to fix what was broken. He was broken. Both mentally and physically. He had the love and acknowledgement from his mother and brother, Hvitserk. But this was different. Elleswith touched his soul and saw the real Ivar for who he was. It was as if someone had come and lit a million candles around him to really highlight who he is. A lonely, seeking, and misunderstood Ivar who could be kind. Sure, Hvitserk and Aslaug saw him and lived around him, loving him for who he was. But Elleswith gave Ivar hope. Hope and reason to be better. More than his family ever saw in him. Listening to Elleswith's melodic voice gave Ivar peace. Made him feel like he didn't wear leg contraptions or that he wasn't weak.

The next morning Elleswith woke up to see Freya gone. Elleswith though was happy that Freya had forgiven her. Freya had said to her that she needed her to see but it went two ways. Elleswith said in her mind: 'Freya, I too need you to see.'

Hvitserk was off talking to Bjorn about some news that had swayed the entire village. The death of the beloved ship master Toki. Bjorn said a stone was to be erected for him, a memorial for all his great deeds in aiding the Vikings. It was eventually erected somewhere. However, the location was unknown to most people. Freya prayed to fair winds that Toki may rest in peace.

Later that day: Ivar was carving wood with a dagger. Freya went to thank Ivar for his advice. Though, knowing that he had been eavesdropping last night, she went to confront him about this.

Freya approached him and said: 'I know you were listening to Elleswith's singing last night.'

Ivar lied: 'I did no such thing.'

Freya scoffed: 'I may be an idiot but through my training as a shield maiden, I've gotten keener senses, I heard your breath loudly.'

Ivar muttered: 'Good for you, Niece.'

Freya sighed: 'Look, stop making this so difficult for both of you. Just tell her how you feel.'

Ivar: 'How can I? She's the wife of my eldest brother Bjorn.'

Freya said: 'Okay whatever.'

She walked away with a grin on her face.

She was cooking up an idea in her mind about how she could get Ivar and Elleswith in one room.

Soon at night: Elleswith was looking at Hastein's shirt. It had, had so much damage that it took awfully long to finish stitching. Freya came back and grabbed the shirt from Elleswith. Elleswith followed after Freya wanting Hastein's shirt back.

Elleswith said while following her out of the great hall: 'Freya please give me the shirt back, besides, you're not supposed to be in the great hall at this hour like this.'

Freya was still grinning. She held the shirt in a way that she beckoned Elleswith to follow her. As Freya reached the room, she passed the shirt to Elleswith and pushed Elleswith into the room.

Elleswith noticed the door closed behind her. She saw Ivar reading something. He had a confused look on his face. Elleswith smiled. She quietly approached him.

She asked: 'Ivar, what are you doing here?

Ivar looked at Elleswith. Lost for words.

Elleswith said: 'We haven't talked for a long time.'

Ivar replied: 'I don't have time for this, please excuse me.'

Freya peeked through the gap in the door. Freya said in her mind:

'Just tell her you moron!' Ivar looked at Elleswith who stood and blocked his way.

Elleswith shook her head and asked the ignorant Ivar: 'Is there something you want to tell me? You've been so distant. We are family now ...'

Elleswith's voice trailed off as Ivar hugged her.

He said: 'I'm sorry.'

Elleswith asked: 'I don't understand, what do you mean?'

Ivar: 'You know what I mean. I'm sorry for feeling so wrongly for my sister-in-law. But I am at a deep end.'

Freya clutched the side of the door with anticipation. She said again in her mind: 'Just tell her you fool!'

Ivar: 'I know that you are not human, I overheard you talking to Freya.'

Elleswith widened her eyes.

Ivar: 'I'm not sure if I'm to believe in elves. Perhaps they do exist. I also know that we are related. Distant cousins. I do not care about any of that. Just know that I will always be there for you. And that none of you will change how I feel for you.'

Ivar sighed, one tear rolling down his cheeks. Freya was surprised. It was the first time she saw Ivar cry.

Ivar: 'Hm, this would be easier for Hvitserk, I'm not good when it comes to emotions, I've always needed to have walls to protect myself. Elleswith, I am in love with you.'

Elleswith was completely confused. Ivar felt this way towards someone for the first time. He kissed her. It was a brief kiss.

Elleswith was even more confused. Freya had covered her eyes. Seeing she was only fifteen, she found it disgusting. Elleswith gently pushed Ivar away and ran out of the room. Past Freya. Ivar saw Freya there.

He frowned angrily and said: 'This was your doing.'

Freya grinned and replied: 'It had to be done Uncle, I could no longer stand your moping.'

A while later that night: Elleswith tried to sleep but couldn't, the memory of that kiss deprived her of her sleep. She pondered over the fact of how Bjorn was with her. Ivar was different. She had felt different at that moment. And she remembered the way they had both looked at each other when they had both met. Elleswith came to the realisation that she felt the exact same way. She snuck out of bed, out of her room, and into Ivar's room which was at the far end of the great hall. Ivar was surprised when he saw Elleswith stand in front of his bed. She climbed into the bed and slept the rest of the night with Ivar in his room. After that, Elleswith and Ivar's bond grew stronger with every emerging day. Elleswith decided to sneak into Ivar's room on an unchecked basis so that no one would notice Elleswith's affair with

Ivar. Elleswith knew that what she was doing seemed somewhat wrong. Sleeping with one of her husband's brothers. But she did not care. For once she put her own feelings first. Freya was happy for Ivar and Elleswith, she willingly protected the secret of their affair. Elleswith truly was in love with Ivar and was not ready to sacrifice that. After all, her marriage to Bjorn had been arranged. He did not care about her, but Ivar did. As long as Aslaug or Bjorn did not discover this, Elleswith would be safe, or so she thought. At the end of this year, Elleswith was helping around in Aslaug's home when suddenly she fainted. Aslaug rushed to break her fall. She laid her on the bed. And leaving Hastein to take care of Elleswith, Aslaug went to talk to Bjorn if Elleswith had been behaving strangely for a while.

Bjorn was drinking some sort of mead when he answered: 'She's been fainting, vomiting a bit, and sleeping a lot, why?'
Aslaug suggested: 'Could Elleswith perhaps be pregnant?'
Bjorn raised his eyebrow. A word he wasn't too fond of.
Aslaug: 'Well if that's the case then you are going to be a father to another child.'
Bjorn: 'Let's just hope not another daughter.'
Aslaug went back to talk to Elleswith. Elleswith felt queasy. Aslaug saw a dazed Elleswith when she broke the possibility to her: 'Elleswith, I've been hearing that you've been feeling under the weather of late. Are you okay?'
Elleswith said in a tired manner: 'No.'
Aslaug said: 'You are with child then.'
Elleswith was a bit shocked. Not so much because she was pregnant but because she did not know who the father was. Since nobody knew about her relations with Ivar, most presumed that the child was Bjorn's. But sadly, she did not know if Ivar or Bjorn was the father.

818 AD
Elleswith was nearly full-term with her child, just one more month. Freya had previously been told with Ivar about the pregnancy. Elleswith had told Ivar the truth. He was the real father. But it couldn't be like that because Bjorn might be suspicious. Bjorn would be led on to believe he was the father of her child. Ivar and Freya were okay with this. Elleswith was watching Hastein clean around her room.

Elleswith laughed and said: 'Foster father, there is no need to do the work of a thrall. You have always been a free man at my side.'
Hastein insisted: 'You are with child, so I'll do the work.'
Freya came in and talked to Elleswith when she saw her father stand across from her. Freya frowned. Bjorn walked up to Freya and looked at her face.

He said: 'You look more and more like your mother. The spitting image of Porunn.'

He went in to talk to Elleswith when Freya said: 'At least I'm not as much like you. I am happy about that.'

Aslaug motioned for Freya to stop.

Freya said in a nasty tone: 'Don't worry, the fool isn't getting to me. He can go bury his face under rocks and sand. Bjorn Stoneside sounds nice.'

Freya walked off. Freya had finished training with the shield maidens for the day when she decided to look for her uncle Sigurd. He was indeed a complicated young man who was now twenty years of age. Still liked travel and gambling over anything else. Sigurd was sitting on a chair at the pub gambling again. He saw Freya approach him. He said sarcastically: 'F-Freya! The successful new shield maiden! Following in your mother's footsteps.'

Freya said while raising her head a bit: 'Shut it! Besides I don't intend to be killed off on a raid like my mother was.'

Sigurd: 'I heard Bjorn got married. And his wife is with child. Tell me, Freya, do you feel like a brother or sister?'

Freya stabbed him with her elbow and sat down next to him. She said: 'Shut it.'

Freya became serious and asked him: 'Why don't you spend time with your real family? Instead of gambling and constant fighting.'

Sigurd grumbled: 'You know that I and Ivar would always fight and compete over the most ridiculous of things, yes? Mother loves Ivar and adores Hvitserk. I'm just the loner, left-out child. I hate fighting with Ivar, we are actually similar. I think when we fight we try to understand each other but it never works out. Mother always followed me about, lecturing me to be nicer. Sadly, that was my way to be nice with Ivar. And I just don't want to burden anyone, so I travel a lot. To keep myself entertained I gamble.'

He grinned and put down a move in his gamble that allowed him to win. Sigurd looked at Freya and said: 'And guess what, I always win.'

Freya smiled a bit. It seemed there was even a part in Sigurd that was hidden and misunderstood. Sigurd talked to Freya about a big raid he'd been planning; a sail down the Mediterranean ocean to a pretty much undiscovered place.

Freya asked: 'So what are the risks of this mission? Why are you including me in this mission?'

Sigurd and Freya walked to the ship docks.

He explained: 'I heard how you fiercely led the battle against the enemy in Mercia, and I have reason to believe that your skills will be of use.'

Freya asked: 'What do you mean?'

Sigurd: 'There have been rumours surfacing that you have a will of Iron. Stronger than that of your father. An adaptable warrior who does not fear fighting in the presence of death.'

Freya went and told Elleswith that she was leaving on a big raid. Sigurd and Freya sailed on a ship with a small army of Vikings and sailed down the Mediterranean ocean. They arrived at a place today known as Spain. Though a small army guarded the place, Freya saw the place and mapped out the entire battle.

She pointed to a hidden trench and said: 'Have foot soldiers hide there. Once the strongest soldiers have fought, the foot soldiers can come out and ambush the rest of the army although if the enemy is strong and our forces are overpowered, we'll have no real good fighters left; have a handful of our best soldiers remain with the foot soldiers. Our archers will go to the raised grassy area there. They can shoot down from the enemies from above. They'll be safe due to the raised height. The enemies won't get there too fast. As for me and you, we'll hide between those trees since we'll be commanding this entire battle, we should go into the enemy first. And we should do this when the guards aren't too aware of anything.'

Sigurd and Freya did as planned. The plan worked like a charm. In a matter of minutes, the entire army that had been guarding the place was gone.

Meanwhile, Elleswith was taking a nap when a strange unknown entity loomed over Elleswith. Elleswith remembered the dark vibes from somewhere. She opened her eyes and screamed. The vampire that was responsible for all the chaos in her life. The vampire grabbed Elleswith by the waist and pulled her off the bed. It bit her. Elleswith tried to move or get away but was completely paralysed. Hastein had heard the commotion and with his secret silver dagger that he had kept hidden from all for this very incident he moved swiftly and stabbed the vampire in the heart. The vampire looked at Hastein. The vampire let go of Elleswith and was struggling to breathe. With a shaking hand, the vampire tried to reach out to its slayer. The vampire burned away bit by bit and eventually vanished. Just gone. Hastein cleaned off the dagger and hid it away again. He asked the half-conscious Elleswith: 'Are you alright?'

Elleswith shook her head.

She said in a faint voice: 'I feel sick.'

Hastein helped Elleswith back on the bed. Aslaug came later to check on Elleswith. She found out from Hastein that Elleswith was suffering from a fever. A bad one at that. The best healer and seer in all of Kattegat, Frode, did not know what to do or how to help the king's wife.

Two days passed, and Freya returned from the raid. Talking to Sigurd all the way back to the great hall. He commended Freya's excellent battle formation skills and said she would make a fine shield maiden. Perhaps live over the reputation of the greatest shield maiden to ever exist, Lagertha. However, Freya had heard that the existence of the famed shield maiden was based on nothing but old fables of the Vikings. Freya went to see Elleswith to tell her of yet another victory. She found Elleswith on the bed and only half conscious.

Aslaug and Bjorn as for Ivar and Hvitserk were gathered around the bed. Along with a familiar face, Frode, the seer. Freya remembered the face of the seer. There was a time when she had been little and snuck off from her grandmother she accidentally went into a shrine. She looked up at a statue.

A voice said: 'Dear child, that is the goddess Freya you gaze upon. She is beautiful, yes, but also strong.'

The little girl turned around to see a man in a hooded garment.

He had a scarred face.

He asked the little girl: 'Now what would someone around your age do here?'

The girl did not answer.

He shook her hand and said: 'My name is Frode, I serve the goddess, Freya.'

'It seems the goddess has gained yet another admirer.'

Flashback ended. Freya never really saw Frode again.

Frode turned to see Freya standing there.

He said in a surprised tone: 'Ah Asa, long time no see.'

Freya frowned and replied: 'It's Freya now.'

Frode nodded.

Aslaug told Freya what was wrong.

The next few days were exhausting.

All Lothbroks waited endlessly till Elleswith recovered. Most began to doubt the possibility of her recovery. Soon after the doubt, Elleswith recovered thanks to Frode and the child was unharmed. Elleswith continued with her life as if nothing had happened. Hastein knew Elleswith was pretending to not remember the incident with the vampire. But it did not matter. The vampire was gone. Elleswith was safe and in less than a month, she was going to have her child.

After Elleswith had given birth, Bjorn sat in the adjoined room feeling like he wanted to rip his hair out. Freya remained a wide distance from her father. A tense atmosphere, all waiting to hear the news of the child.

Ivar distracted himself by talking to Hvitserk. Aslaug stared at the ceiling.

Suddenly a thrall opened the door and said: 'It's a boy.'

Bjorn could not believe his ears. He had finally gotten the son he always wanted. Bjorn went to hold 'his' son. Elleswith was just happy the birth went smoothly. Freya rolled her eyes. If only her father knew the truth. That baby he held was not her brother but a cousin. Celebrations went on for weeks on end now that Bjorn had his heir. The heir was named Oliver Lothbrok. Freya saw Elleswith happy with her son. Freya was content though having seen Frode after such a long time made her curious enough to go and talk to him. Freya went to talk to Frode at the temple of Freya in Kattegat. She found Frode sweeping the floor inside the dim-lit isolated building. He looked up to see Freya.

He greeted her: 'Hello Freya, I believe I still have to get used to your new name.'

Freya said to him: 'It was so long ago that I last came here. Now I'm sixteen.'

Frode said: 'It is when we truly acknowledge time itself when we begin to notice how many things have come to pass.'

Freya looked at the gentle face of the goddess.

She remarked: 'You know, the goddess Freya isn't that beautiful.'

Frode said with a smile: 'It is not the beauty but the heart.'

He went on to say: 'Freya was one of the most talented amongst the gods. And one of the only women. But it was her power and graceful nature that made her loved. But her legacy is long forgotten now. She has the occasional admirers.'

Freya had always been attached to the goddess. The one that had also inspired her own name long before Elleswith mentioned to change names.

Freya said: 'No, Freya is a great goddess, what about all her ancient legends, the battle of Ymir?'

Frode said in a surprised tone: 'So, you know the old tales, the tales most Norse folk lack to know. I am surprised.'

Freya said: 'Say thanks to my Uncle Hvitserk, he taught me to read the old Norse texts that document the old stories of the gods. I read most of them. The story of Yggdrasil was by far the most interesting.'

Frode asked in an honest tone: 'Don't you think there lies some truth in the ancient stories?'

Freya: 'You mean Yggdrasil really existed?'

Frode: 'The tree of life, is the Yggdrasil, the tree the ancients guarded with their lives. It is strongly rumoured to have existed.'

Freya heard the word: ancients. She remembered how Elleswith had said that she was one of the last pure descendants of the ancients. Freya asked herself: Were the ancients all elven creatures? Are there still things Elleswith hides from me? If elves exist, then perhaps Yggdrasil really did exist as well.

She asked Frode: 'Frode, could you teach me more about the Norse folklore?'

Frode: 'Of course, I have been looking for an apprentice for a long time.'

Freya stepped back and said: 'Um, apprentice? I have to be an apprentice to a seer and be a shield maiden at the same time?'

Frode: 'If you want the knowledge, you must swear an oath to the temple of Freya. Doing so will initiate a path for you as a Gydia in the near future, if you happen to remain in the service of the goddess Freya.'

Freya: 'No, I don't intend to become a priestess.'

Seventeen years later, 835 AD, Kattegat

It was sixteen years from the death of Bjorn Lothbrok, having died a year after his son Oliver was born. After forming the great Vaeringjar army (army of the sworn men), he fought alongside his brother Sigurd and the army against the Northumbrians. Sigurd had died on the battlefield and Bjorn was fatally wounded. The battle was lost, he returned to Kattegat and died there later on. Bjorn got a Viking funeral. They put his body on a small ship and let it sail on the water. Aslaug shot a burning arrow at the ship. The ship went up in flames. After the funeral, the soldiers were ordered to bring the ashes to the house of Munso, the allied forces of the house of Lothbrok. These allied forces were on an island named Munso in a place called Ekero (the house of Munso was the ancestral house of Lothbrok, the descendants later came to rule over Norway via Ragnar Lothbrok). Having always trusted his relatives in Munso more than his own family, Bjorn willed upon his demise and had his ashes be sent into a memorial somewhere in his original homeland. His memorial was placed in Lake Malaren in Ekero in Sweden (this memorial actually exists still but the stone is quite broken). Freya did not care about her father being dead. In fact, a part of her rejoiced in his death. Oliver was not even a toddler at the time. He was not able to rule in his father's stead. And so, Aslaug became regent alongside Hvitserk and Elleswith till Oliver was of age.

Now back to the present story seventeen years later in 835 AD: Aslaug began to prepare herself for retirement. Hvitserk was thirty-nine years of age and his work as an advisor to the next ruler had just begun. Ivar prepared the young seventeen-year-old Oliver for what lay in store for him. Freya was thirty-three now and had joined the great Vaeringjar army and became a Gydia (from the Norse language for priestess). Aslaug still mourned the death of her two sons, especially over Sigurd. The problem child she had scolded her whole life but never forgave herself for trying to understand him. Ivar who was thirty-eight years of age pretended to not care over Sigurd's death but remembered all the times they fought and threw food at Ragnar. It seems that Aslaug could no longer deal with all the death and the misfortune in her family. She poisoned herself. Upon the discovery of Aslaug's death, she was buried in a secret place. It was rumored that she was buried in the place where she and Ragnar had first met. After this, one day, Freya and Frode were sitting in front of the statue reading ancient texts. Freya had once learned more about the battle of Ymir. The ancients went and fought against a great storm of a giant. Sacrificing their lives to protect all at the expense of a few, they fell and scattered across the human continents never seen nor heard of again. Apparently, in Christian belief, they believe that there is one god, whereas the ancients were multiple god-like creatures created by a higher being. Frode had told Freya that the goddess Freya served in the battle of Ymir alongside all others. And after the battle, she became recognised as a true goddess, and the giant Ymir was destroyed. Freya learned today the historical aftermath of Ymir. Freya looked at the scroll she held; she saw old inscriptions and an old drawing of the battle of Ymir. She remembered a similar drawing from the elven saga she had read. The ancients had pointed ears much like Elleswith but had wings. This did indeed confirm her theory of the ancients being elves.

She asked Frode: 'Do the elves from the elven saga have relations to the battle of Ymir?'

Frode pointed at the old drawing on the scroll which Freya held and said: 'I suppose they do, after the battle of Ymir, Ymir's leftover magic created the dark elven, the savages of the earth.'

Freya: 'Aren't they referred in Christian biblical things as demons?'

Frode said: 'Yes and the ancients have high relevance to the beings called angels.'

Freya became even more curious. So, there was more that Elleswith hid from her.

Later: Freya wanted to talk to Elleswith and ask her one thing: Did the story of Ymir have relations to the family of Yanmir? Ymir and Yanmir could nearly be the same name so maybe there was a connection between the two. On the way there she saw Oliver practice throwing knives at a tree stump.

She went over and asked Ivar: 'What are you both doing here?'

Ivar: 'Well, Oliver isn't too good at throwing axes - yet.'

Oliver turned around, frowned, and said: 'I'm not like my strong armed father.'

Ivar raised his eyebrow. He grinned slightly.

Oliver noticed this; he asked in an annoyed tone: 'What's so humorous?'

Freya smiled.

She said: 'You'll find out one day, brother.'

Ivar lectured Oliver: 'Keep your feet flat on the floor, hold the dagger-like this, stop with the eye-squinting. Oliver, closing your eyes won't help you.'

Oliver lied: 'Hey, I'm not going to close my eyes.'
Freya saw Oliver finally get one dagger thrown at the target.
Ivar commended him: 'Good, now keep doing that, and eventually,
once you've mastered this skill, you can pick up a bow and arrow.'
Oliver was a lot like Ivar, his real father (Oliver did not know that
Ivar was his real father). Overly serious and uptight as well as a sturdy
personality, but considerate to those around him and sympathetic. He
had a low patience drive but had relative control over it. Though the one
difference between Ivar and Oliver was that Ivar was more of a toughy
and a natural-born fighter and loved fighting but that was only because
he was bullied by others. Ivar also had a more robust personality. Freya
saw that all as the two worked together. Freya went to go see Elleswith.
Elleswith saw Freya approach her. Elleswith had been cleaning up
Aslaug's old home. Now that Aslaug was dead, there was no need of this
house to be in its current filled state. It only carried memories of
sadness.
As Freya helped Elleswith clean out the place she asked Elleswith:
'Does the battle of Ymir have relations to your family of Yanmir?'
Elleswith asked: 'Did you learn this in your studies as a Gydia?'
Freya nodded.
Elleswith said: 'There lies truth, but the story of Ymir isn't all that
true. For example, the demons were not created by the magic of Ymir,
that part of the true story was falsified by the Scandinavian people. The
demons existed long before the story of Ymir was even written. And
Ymir did not even exist, that is a creature created by what the
Scandinavian people thought had happened. The allmother was the one
that brought the wrath onto the ancients because the ancients had done
something to enrage their creator. The wrath was the giant storm not a
giant in the storm. The old Norse folk weren't being literal.'
Freya laughed a bit.
Elleswith continued to say: 'As for your question if my family has
ties to the event of Ymir, no. Yanmir was the one to write down the
event in old Norse, they called the great storm after their own family.
Hence the name Ymir, Yanmir.'
Freya sighed in relief. Elleswith and Freya continued to empty
the home.

Later that day: Freya went to see how Oliver was doing. Oliver had
wrapped up training for the day.
He was eating a piece of bread. Freya sat down next to him and
said: 'I feel sorry for you, brother.'
Oliver asked: 'Why? You rarely feel sorry for anyone. Let alone me.'
Freya shoved him.
His bread fell out of his hand.
She scowled: 'Give me a break! I'm not like that! Is that really

what you think of me!'

Oliver yelled back: 'Will you stop yelling, I still need my ears thanks!'

Freya scoffed: 'Ach, fine you're right, my personality is very complex.'

Oliver smirked and said: 'And I'm right because I finally got you to admit it. You idiot.'

Freya shouted: 'Me idiot, yeah we'll see about that!' She ruffled his hair.

He complained, telling her to stop. Hvitserk came outside.

He said: 'Nephew, it's time for your language lessons.'

Oliver became serious again and said: 'Alright.'

He said to Freya: 'We'll continue this conversation another time, there are many things we must discuss, things I never really got to tell you, so until next time, sister.'

Freya shook her head.

Then she asked herself: What could be so important that he couldn't tell me now?

The next day, Freya went to her lesson with Frode since there were currently no wars or raids. Strangely the song that Elleswith had sung to her once was stuck in her head. She hummed the tune as she worked. Frode noticed the familiar lyrics and asked Freya what she was singing. She sang it out aloud for Frode. Frode hurried to grab an old book. He placed it on a giant stone and blew the dust off it. He showed her an old song labelled the prophecy of light. The lyrics were: As all stars fall, many dozen big and small. A hope that had been born, now forlorn. Light scatters across the vast veil, piercing the heart of the belief that good would always prevail. In the white light, with eyes open wide, awaken and embrace the new days before it is lost again in thy ways. Freya was amazed to see the song that Elleswith had sung both to her and Oliver in this book.

Frode asked: 'So, where did you hear this song?'

Freya remembered she would protect Elleswith's secret and so she answered: 'I forgot where.'

Frode sighed in a disappointed manner and said: 'Such a shame, such an old song.'

Freya asked: 'What is a shame?'

Frode said: 'Hmm well, this book has been in here ever since this temple was built but I can't seem to discover the point of this song. Everything else I understand but this one song is a mystery. Nobody knows who wrote this book. Not even the seers who came before me. I hoped you could help me but even you do not know anything, let alone the origins of this song.'

Freya suggested: 'Maybe look into the elven sagas, it is said there that the ancients sang countless songs of prophecies to come.'

Frode thanked his apprentice. They did their work to Kattegat when a strange man came and asked for a blessing from the goddess Freya. Freya was asked to aid the man. He seemed to be a Viking fighter. Freya did the necessary ritual to bestow a blessing onto anyone, though this man tried to strike up a conversation with Freya. He said his name was Sinric. He said he worked in the fifth battalion of the Vaeringjar army. Freya said she also was a part-time shield maiden, third battalion of the Vaeringjar army. As Freya told him her name he burst into a fit of laughter.

He said: 'I am being given the blessing of Freya by a Freya! I'm sorry but that's one of the funniest things I've ever heard!'

Freya rolled her eyes and left the temple.

Sinric ran after her and said: 'I'm sorry if I insulted you.'

Freya assured him in a nasty manner: 'Don't worry about it, I'm already used to it by now.'

Freya looked for Oliver in the great hall. He was learning how to address citizen matters. He was quite annoyed by the looks of it. He seemed like he wanted to scrunch up his uncle's letters and throw them at him. But he refrained from doing so. His facial expression changed drastically.

He said: 'Uncle can we continue this another time, there is something I'd like to talk with my sister about.'

Hvitserk walked off. Freya stood there, with an annoyed face. Oliver sat down with Freya and talked to her.

Oliver asked Freya: 'You know mother is of elven blood.'

Freya said: 'Don't say that so openly.'

Oliver: 'I know, sorry. Anyway, I wanted to tell you the truth about me, something Mother hid from all.'

Freya pointed out: 'What's there to tell, you are half-elven and my relative.'

Oliver: 'Yes but –'

Freya: 'What?'

Oliver snapped. He pounded the table with one fist and shouted: 'Like always, you never listen!'

Freya stopped and said: 'Okay, tell me.'

Oliver calmed down and said: 'When Mother said she was fine after recovering from her illness before I was born, she was bitten by a vampire that had chased her here to Kattegat.'

Freya widened her eyes. She muttered angrily: 'She never told me that.'

Oliver said: 'Yes, she did not tell me either, Hastein told me. After she was bitten by the vampire, she fell ill but recovered thanks to her elven blood. However, the illness from the vampire had certain side effects on me. The vampire's bite was enough to turn me into a vampire but since I was not directly turned I survived and became a half-vampire and half-elven.'

Freya laughed and said: 'I believe you that vampires exist but you're joking that half-vampire. Please tell me you're joking.'

Oliver smirked and said: 'It seems you don't believe me.'

He grabbed his dagger which lay on the table and in a quick cut he slit the palm of his hand. He put aside his blood-smeared weapon and showed his sister the palm of his hand. Normally Freya wasn't squeamish but watching the wound close by itself was, well, weird. Freya blinked multiple times. From seeing magical healing powers from Elleswith to self-healing wounds from her brother, it kind of creeped her out.

Freya shouted: 'Ooookay, that's enough!'

Oliver sat back in his chair and cleaned the dagger's blade. He asked her with a humorous look: 'Believe me now?'

Freya nodded but out of curiosity she asked: 'Do you have a weakness to sunlight?'

Oliver: 'No, my elven side allows me to walk in sunlight and mirrors, that old myth is fake.'

Freya asked: 'How do you know?'

Oliver: 'When you are of demon species you know stuff like that.'

Freya said: 'No wonder Elleswith is against you going on the battlefield. And Uncle Ivar, does he know?'

Oliver replied: 'Yes, that's why he trains me, not someone else. Ivar and Mother said that once I finished training, I will never go onto the battlefield.'

Freya said: 'Imagine a Viking that heals. All of Kattegat would either think you a god or a monster.'

Oliver joked: 'I have no wish to be either.'

Freya felt like she understood her brother more.

A month later in this year, Freya heard conflict arising in Sweden under the rule of King Harald fair hair (some sources say Bjorn Ironside had been the king of Sweden and Harald the king of Norway, but others say Bjorn had no rule over Sweden and more rule over Norway). King Harald who had always been a friend of Ragnar's and took care of the house of Munso wanted to overthrow the accession to the throne of Oliver Lothbrok. A war was silently brewing. A war that had the high possibility of being worse than the one against the Northumbrians. Freya started to prepare for the potential war. Oliver had also heard King Harald's hatred towards him. He was not even king of Norway yet and someone already questioned him. Hvitserk and Elleswith who were acting as regents ordered the great Vaeringjar army to prepare themselves. As Harald moved with his forces to the frontier of Norway, it was up to the greatest army in Norway to make a stand. The sixth battalion was sent out to map out the current situation. Only half of that battalion returned. It became clear to the folk of Kattegat that Harald was not bluffing. He was serious in this all-out war. It was either fight or die. Freya powdered her hands in ashes and covered her face with a symbol of her enduring fighting spirit. She said her farewells to all. The third and fifth battalions of the army gathered at the frontier, fighting alongside the remaining Vikings of the sixth battalion. Freya discovered that the man she had bestowed a blessing upon back at the temple, Sinric, was the leader of the fifth group. His full name was Sinric von Halfdan. He spoke with the leader of Freya's battalion of the Skjaldmaer (old Norse for shield maiden). Sinric saw Freya and shook hands with her. They looked at the battlefield and knew in an instant that the battle could go both ways.

Freya and her allies ran onto the battlefield. Freya hit her axe against her round wooden shield. The Vikings fought with all their might. They drove back what was left of the Swedish forces. The remaining Swedes retreated while they still had the chance.

The army of Vikings raised their weapons and celebrated the victory. Freya stood in the middle of the field, she panted, completely drained. She had a hunch that the Swedes would return with more fighting power. More than what Freya had experienced just now. The two battalions returned victoriously. Sinric and Freya formed a partnership. Sinric said he looked forward to fighting alongside the skjaldmaer battalion. Freya began to trust Sinric like a friend. The battles though had only just begun. Then there came a man named Erik Bjornsson. He claimed to be the rightful heir to the throne of Kattegat and Norway. Erik was detained for his false claims. Ivar said that this Erik was a bastard son of Bjorn and a spy sent by Harald to help infiltrate Kattegat. The security increased around Kattegat. Meanwhile, Harald was setting up a deal with the king of Francia. Harald got extra soldiers and the king of Francia got a part of Sweden in return. Harald took his forces to the frontier for the last battle. All of the Vaeringjar armies gathered at the frontier to fight off the Swedes and foreign soldiers. Under the commands of Ivar, the battalions commenced. Though Ivar watched back in horror as all the Vikings who were drained from fighting against the fallen Swedes were now being overpowered by Harald's remaining forces. Ivar hated that the greatest army in all of Norway was being brought to its knees. Freya who was one of the last soldiers standing alongside Sinric waited for Ivar's command. Ivar looked at Freya. He saw at this moment a grown woman and remembered the little girl she had once been. One of the only friends he had ever had. One of the only people he had learned kindness from. He made a decision. One someone should never have to make.

He shouted at the two surviving soldiers: 'Retreat!'

Ivar forced his way with his broken legs into the lion's den.
For the first time, Freya felt the ravages of war clutch her heart.

She yelled: 'No, don't do it! Uncle! Uncle Ivar! Nooooo!'
Ivar collapsed to the ground not before wounding some of the
enemies. His weapon fell down next to him. He lay there. A lifeless
corpse. Sinric had pulled Freya to the ship. They returned to Kattegat.
Freya left Sincric and in a fit of rage, she went to the great hall. She
yelled at Hvitserk who was discussing battle strategies with Oliver.
Freya: 'Ivar is dead, what do you have to say to this! You are here and
chattering about, meanwhile, we're out there being killed off! Cowards!'
She made a strong fist and intended to punch Hvitserk. Freya
scrunched her face, she began to cry. Hvitserk had never seen this
side of Freya.
Freya: 'I–I watched him die.'
Hvitserk said trying to give his niece some solace: 'This is the cost
of war. Losing the ones we love.'
Later: Harald had Ivar's body sent to Kattegat as a message that the
war was not over yet. Not by a long shot. Elleswith was completely
shocked. Ivar was given a Viking funeral. Freya shot a flaming arrow
at the ship. The ship was being engulfed by the fire. Freya lowered
the bow and gazed at the flaming ship. She remembered all the times
Aslaug and her two uncles had sat around a table and eaten together.
Freya clenched her teeth. She said to herself: Oh no, I'm not going
to cry. Ivar's sarcastic laugh lingered in her mind.
She said: 'Goodbye.'

At night, all could not rest. Freya forced herself to stay awake.
Elleswith buried her face in her blanket. In the meantime, Oliver
went to check on the detained prisoner, Erik Bjornsson. The cell was
open. Oliver had a shiver sent down his spine. He ran to look for
the unpredictable Viking. Erik was trying to escape from Kattegat.
Elleswith who had been taking a walk outside due to her unrest stood
in front of the dark figure. That dark figure was a bit shaken at the
sight of someone else. He acted fast and without mercy. He stabbed
the oblivious person using a silver dagger he had found after his escape
from his cell. Freya who was doing night patrol in the immediate event of
an invasion, heard someone scream. It was a shrill scream. Freya rushed
to the area as she recognised the voice. It had been Elleswith screaming
out. But it was too late.

Elleswith lay flat on the floor on her stomach surrounded by a
puddle of blood. Elleswith who looked up with her weak eyes reached
out to the opposing person standing in front of her. Freya ran and knelt
next to her. Her clothing got soaked in blood. Freya turned
Elleswith around and rested her head on her lap.
Freya stammered: 'N–no, this isn't fair.'

Elleswith tried to say something but coughed. She coughed up blood.

Elleswith said in a frail tone: 'Nothing is fair Freya. In the eye of truth, there is nothing you can do. Neither for me nor Ivar.'
Freya shook her head. She put her hand on Elleswith's wound to put pressure on it.
She said: 'I will not lose you too.'
Elleswith coughed again and said: 'Death is something one cannot escape. I–I'm sorry Freya. I should've fought back. Just that Ivar is dead, I could not find the will to fight.'
Freya asked: 'You were attacked?'
Freya demanded: 'By whom!?'
Elleswith raised her hand to Freya's cheek and said: 'It does not matter. Nothing matters right now but the last words I wish to bestow upon you.'
Elleswith said: 'I have lived a good life. I have no regrets. Please tell Hastein to let go. Freya, please forgive me. And don't forget to hold your head high, I suppose I changed my mind, you are an idiot, but ... You are not the type of idiot you think yourself.'
Freya laughed.
Elleswith said: 'That's the way, try to be at peace with yourself.'
Freya's laugh vanished as she saw the life fade away from her.
Elleswith had closed her eyes and simply stopped moving. Elleswith's arm slid out of Freya's grasp and onto the ground. Freya leaned over her friend.
She pleaded: 'I wish you could sing again for me one last time.'
A voice said: 'I will sing you a song. One last time.'

The voice sang the song. Freya closed her eyes and cried. Oliver approached Freya and saw what had happened. He hugged Freya. Hastein came and carried the body away. She was buried in a place atop a hill in Kattegat where the sun shined the most.
Freya watched over the burial with Hastein when she said to him: 'Elleswith told me to tell you to let go.'
She asked: 'What did she mean by that?'
Hastein pulled a torn bit of fabric from his bag.
He sighed and explained: 'She meant to let go of the past of what I lost. And to let go of her.'
He said: 'It is my time to leave.'
Hastein walked past Freya as if she were a ghost. He left Kattegat later that day. Oliver did not speak to Freya. Freya stayed in Kattegat that day. Having lost so many, she no longer knew what to do. Sinric went to inform her of reports of Harald's army. Apparently, Harald raided many smaller towns in Norway. The army could strike Kattegat at any moment.
Freya yelled at him: 'How are we supposed to make a stand now with all of our forces depleted?'

Sinric: 'We can only hope that that does not happen.'
Freya scowled: 'Vikings shouldn't pray! I'm so fed up with hope!'
Sinric grabbed Freya by the wrist.
He said: 'Listen, I just want you to know that I will fight with you
still. You will always have been my rival and friend, that I promise
you if I die.'
He let go of her wrist and walked away. Meanwhile, Erik Bjornsson
had tracked down his leader, Harald. Erik planned to help Harald
infiltrate Kattegat.
Harald had received the map of the secret route into Kattegat
from Erik and said: 'You fool, you really thought I would give you
the throne to Norway! Pah, I have no more need for you. A traitor
to his own people.'
He took his great axe and eradicated Erik on the spot.
Harald told his followers: 'We travel now and fight at sunset, let's
move!'

At sunset, Harald and his men arrived at the walls of Kattegat.
The watchers that looked over the walls in towers yelled: 'Enemies
approaching!'
A horn was blown. Freya heard the horn blow. She ran up to
Sinric. Together they ran up to the barrier walls and climbed up
the ladder. They looked down to see the horde of soldiers under
Harald's command.
Harald's voice boomed as he announced: 'Stand down or be prepared
to die. I will show no mercy to those who stand in my way.'
Sinric looked at Freya and whispered: 'He's bluffing.'
Freya nodded and yelled: 'No! We will not stand down; we will
never stop fighting!'
Harald shook his head in sadness. He said: 'Very well then, die it is.'
At this, a huge number of enemy Vikings came in like a flood.
Freya looked down in disbelief. She couldn't understand how Harald's
army was able to break into Kattegat unnoticed.
Freya yelled: 'Brace yourselves Vikings, fight to the death for that
is all we can do.'

Sinric took a last look at Harald. Harald though was no longer
there. Sinric grabbed a shield and weapon alongside Freya, though all
inside Kattegat was surrendering. The villagers surrendered, meanwhile
the remaining Vikings had been cut down.
Freya had a troublesome thought run through her head: 'Oliver!'
Freya had lost focus for a brief moment and left herself wide open
for an attack. The attacker wielded their axe against Freya. Luckily,

Sinric ran in behind her and held the shield into which the axe clashed with. Freya and Sinric were now standing back-to-back against each other, surrounded by angry looking Swedes.

Freya said: 'Sinric, this is a suicide mission.'

He said out loud: 'I know; so, any plans Freya?'

Freya saw a strange foreign-looking man. He had some weird presence around him which made Freya feel insecure. His face was hidden. Somehow Freya's vision was very hazy. He smiled. A very twisted smile. He raised a finger to his lips as if to signify silence to her. He raised one hand towards the enemies and froze them all on the spot.

Sinric said while running through the crowd of enemies: 'It seems the decision has been made for us! I don't get what just happened but let's go find your uncle and brother!'

Freya shook her head twice.

The figure was gone now.

Freya followed after Sinric. Sinric and Freya ran to the great hall to find an injured Hvitserk outside. Hvitserk was badly wounded. Freya knelt down beside him and asked: 'What happened? Uncle?'

Hvitserk moaned in pain and handed her a piece of paper. It was stained with blood from his wound.

He said in a weak tone: 'You must find Oliver; he was apprehended by Harald. Please find him before it is too late.'

Freya: 'Uncle, what is this map?'

Hvitserk looked at Freya, there was a sadness in his eyes.

He said: 'I'm sorry for never telling you. This whole war, I could have prevented all of-of t-this.'

Freya squeezed his hand and said: 'Uncle, it's not your fault. Uncle!'

Hvitserk died. Freya stood up.

She shook her head and replied: 'Goodbye.'

Freya opened up the note that Hvitserk had passed to her. In it, tucked away, were various other notes. Fragile paper, Freya was careful in handling it. One was a letter in Hvitserk's handwriting, it said:

Dear family, if you are reading this now, I am dead or something terrible has taken place. Having always been Bjorn's advisor, I was the one who knew the most of Bjorn's plans and secrets. I was sworn to secrecy this whole time. Please do not hate me. The truth is, Ragnar is not dead. And the reason he went missing in the first place was because of his eldest son Bjorn. After Bjorn became more and more lustful for the throne of Norway, he began to come up with schemes to remove Ragnar from the throne without suspicion from Kattegat or his own family. He stole an ancient document in the library in the great hall and used it to manipulate Ragnar. Ragnar who always wanted nothing more than to discover if he truly had blood ties to Odin. Bjorn lied, while using the old document, that

Odin lived in the magical underwater realm of Atlantis. The
myths were actually that Poseidon resided there and not Odin.
Ragnar was foolish enough to believe this. And so hence the
disappearance of Ragnar. Bjorn had a random assassin sent
after Ragnar in secret just to make sure that Ragnar would
not return to Kattegat either way. For a long time, Harald
suffered under the loss of his best friend Ragnar. Not only
his friend but the man he had sworn an oath to. That oath
was to guard the throne of Sweden as regent no matter what
and fealty towards Ragnar. Since Ragnar was related to the
house of Munso but too distant, he was unable to be the king
of Sweden, so he took to the throne of Norway. And with that
new regal power, he appointed Harald as regent over Sweden.
That is all I know about Harald's connection to Ragnar.
After a long time, Bjorn felt the hatred from the Swedish king.
He did not want to be involved in any war against Harald
and so he built a secret passageway in and out of Kattegat.
There is an attached map. It is only a copy. The original was
stolen by someone who probably gave it to Harald by now.
Freya finished reading and looked at a strange drawing, an old
depiction of what was called Atlantis. Freya saw faint writing in the
corner of the drawing. It roughly said, written in Norse: Is Odin
there? Need to know.
Must find Odin. Signed, Ragnar Lothbrok.

It was squiggly handwriting.
The writing of a fanatic in pursuit of the unknown. Freya understood
now a bit more of why Harald was doing what he was doing. Out of
honour and respect for the oath he had made to a best friend. Freya
though did not care for the reason. She only knew now that all of
her family was dead and that if Oliver was not found, she would have
no one left. That was the hard truth she was forced to face. Freya
used the map and with Sinric, she headed to the secret passageway.
Though what she did not know was that an enemy hid, in waiting. It
was a long tunnel outstretched underneath Kattegat with only weak
torches to light the path ahead. She saw, at the far end of the tunnel,
Oliver unconscious on the moist ground.
Harald stood, holding his great axe over Oliver. When he saw
Freya and Sinric approach, he held his weapon up in their direction
and said in angered tone: 'What must it take for me to get the truth!
Do you fools think I like waging wars? No. I had hoped that the
granddaughter and other sons would understand. I had hoped that
Freya Lothbrok would side with me and her uncles to overthrow the
lunatic Bjorn Ironside. I lost the man I trusted the most.'
Freya yelled: 'I lost everyone else because of your so-called noble
cause! You are a fool! Bjorn lied to us all! And Ragnar was foolish

enough to believe his son's lies in the first place!'

Harald's voice boomed: 'You know nothing about Ragnar! Stop talking!'

Freya silenced herself. Oliver woke up. His eyes were the colour of charcoal.

Oliver tiredly asked Freya: 'What's going on here?'

Freya looked at Oliver and then back at the vile Harald.

Oliver's eyes darted at Harald.

He said: 'So, you are the one who knocked me over from behind.'

Harald saw Oliver's eyes.

He screeched: 'Eeeeeeehya, what are you!?!'

Oliver chuckled and said in a sly manner: 'None of your concern.'

Harald crept back from Oliver who closed in on him. Oliver did nothing but scare that Viking with his irregular eye colour. Harald accidentally tripped over a boulder and fell to the ground on his backside.

His axe well ... Oliver looked away. Freya shook her head at the Viking who had been killed by his own weapon.

Oliver said: 'Whoa, talk about stupid deaths.'

He pulled the axe from Harald and tossed it aside.

The weapon made a clang sound as it hit the ground.

Freya shook her head and said: 'Stop with the morbid madness.'

Oliver: 'What, I was only stating facts.'

Freya said: 'Well, good to know that you're okay.'

Oliver was about to reply when a horde of Vikings came running down the tunnel.

Sinric yelled: 'Freya, we have to evacuate immediately!'

Freya nodded in agreement, when she turned to leave, she saw the other side of the tunnel barricaded by three Vikings. Sinric was attacked by an enemy. He was badly wounded and collapsed to the ground.

Freya yelled: 'Sinric, can you stand?'

Sincric grinned at Freya. It was a grin of pain.

He said to Freya seconds before the enemy closed in on him: 'Freya, the greatest weapon of a Viking is to fight towards a goal and always survive battles at the expense of a few.'

He nodded at Freya and shouted in a furious tone: 'Go, you know what you must do! Do not stay behind for a timewaster. Remember what I said to you, that if I die, I promised to you that I will always have considered you my greatest rival and ally.'

Freya saw Sinric block the enemy's path by acting as an obstacle. His right eye was slashed by a sword. Sinric shouted out in pain. Freya nodded and, having taken down the three opposing Vikings that blocked the exit with Oliver, they escaped into the night. Oliver and Freya escaped Kattegat that night and did not return. Freya believed in Sinric's promise. Even though she felt sad about losing a comrade, she was also proud to have known someone so dignified and loyal for a Viking. Freya and Oliver arrived in a small village.

There was an old, abandoned farmhouse in which they both stayed for the night. Freya though had an incessant pain in her left hip. Oliver saw Freya remove what was covering the wound.

Oliver complained: 'Freya, why didn't you tell me you were hurt! This is a really bad wound. You could die if it doesn't heal. Freya! Are you even listening! You've already lost a lot of blood. How long have you hid this wound from me? I could heal this with my elven powers.'

Freya pretended to be fine.

She said: 'No, I'll be alright. I -' Freya was unable to finish her sentence when she collapsed to the ground. Unconscious.

Oliver yelled: 'Sister!'

Oliver yelled multiple times, but Freya did not hear him. The voice was muffled out just like the light. There was nothing but a vast void in Freya's mind. She looked left, then right, nothing. She ran forth but ended back where she had been before. Time passed. She could not tell how much. She felt like with every second, she was growing more and more tired, till ground shook beneath her, forcing her to return to the world of the living. It was like someone opened the door to a bright sun to someone who was tired. Oliver saw Freya's eyelids tremble. Then she sat upright, in shock.

Oliver said: 'It worked. Freya, I'm sorry, for a moment there you had me worried.'

Freya stammered: 'W-what h-happened?'

Oliver said in a nervous tone: 'Freya, you nearly died. If I hadn't brought you back ...'

Freya grabbed his collar and furiously yelled: 'What did you do!!!! DID IT LOOK LIKE I WAS SUFFERING! WELL?'

Oliver frowned and hit her hand away.

He said in an angered tone: 'I did what I had to do. I'm sorry that if turning you into a vampire brings you misery. Do you think I was ready to lose the last family I have left?'

Freya complained: 'I lost everything and gave my last to save you. I'm a Viking Oliver, I had been prepared to die since the days I became a shield maiden in the first place! Why didn't you let me die!'

She balled her hands into tight fists.

Oliver: 'Were you that ready to die? Why did you even want to save me in the first place? If you wanted to die so badly, why were you afraid to lose me? You know Freya, you're too complicated to understand sometimes.'

Freya succumbed to a mass headache. She knelt down on the floor and screeched.

Oliver: 'Since I was a born vampire, I didn't suffer like you do now.'

Freya glared angrily at Oliver. She threw a chair at him. He dodged it with ease.

She yelled: 'I, go, I don't want to see you!'

Oliver looked at her. A sad expression on his face. He shook his head and with the vampiric speed, he left the room.

Oliver left and wandered back to Kattegat. He visited his mother's grave when he was approached by a stranger. The stranger removed his cloaking spell and revealed his identity. His voice was loud and clear. He said to Oliver: 'So, you are one of the demons behind this entire scenario.'

Oliver's eyes widened as he asked: 'H-how do you know what I am?'

The stranger introduced himself: 'My name is Lucien. I believe you are Oliver Lothbrok. Come with me now, we have much to talk about regarding the capitol offence that was directed at your mother.' Lucien's blue eyes burned intensely at Oliver.

Oliver coughed. Lucien held his hand out to Oliver.

Lucien said: 'Sorry for that, there is still much for me to learn when it comes to controlling my powers, I too am a demon.'

Oliver felt like he could trust the man and remembered what Freya had said to him earlier: 'I, go, I don't want to see you!'

He followed Lucien through an odd-looking door. After they went through, the door vanished behind them.

The next morning, Freya had fallen asleep. When she woke up, she had burns all over her body. The rays of sunlight were burning her skin. She shuffled out of the sunlight that filtered in through the one window. Freya realised that this was her life now. Forever, since vampires were immortal. Freya felt so weak. At night she went hunting to satisfy her need for blood from animals. She did so till she could bear it no more. She took the silver dagger she had stolen from Hastein and intended to drive it through her heart. She could not even make the tip of the dagger come in contact with her heart. A strange force prevented her from doing so.

After a while, time passed, and she no longer cared about her sanity and became a true barbarian. One night she visited a meadow near Kattegat that she had played in with her uncles when she had been little. It brought back so many memories that it reminded Freya of herself. Who she had been. Strong, independent, and an idiot. Now she was a killer and an idiot. She had nothing left and like always, like her father, she only cared about herself and pushed others away as long as it benefited herself. Truly she was an idiot. She was dead. She had always been dead.

Maybe being a vampire was the fitting ending for her. Suddenly, she saw a light shimmer in the distance.

A voice sang ever so beautifully: 'A path that is treacherous, light a fire and seek what lies ahead. The path that you light to see is yours and yours alone as a soul sings this song. A heart forged in darkness is not strength but sadness, all surrounded by madness. Light is too frail and in fail. In both, though there is always a choice and a reason no matter how or what. Raise your head as the path you take is yours and find a balance.'

Freya looked about. She recognised the song.
Freya shouted out: 'Elleswith!'
A strong gust of wind blew. Freya saw Elleswith hold out her hand.
She smiled and said: 'I sang you the last piece of the song. Freya, be strong no matter the fool you are, for that is you.'
Ivar appeared next to Elleswith as well as Hvitserk and Aslaug and Sigurd. Ivar glared angrily at Sigurd. Hvitserk went in between his two brothers. Aslaug smirked.
Sigurd waved to Freya as he said: 'It seems as I gambled in life, death had gambled with me.'
Ivar: 'Do not waste the lessons I have given you, Freya.'
Freya watched as the essence of the spirits faded away. Freya began to cry.
She said: 'Okay.'
Freya did raise her head and chose a path. She decided to live life like her grandfather had done before he had become ruler of Kattegat. She became a farmer who specialised in whatever her farm soil managed to grow. Life was hard, especially when she tended to the crops at night. She once accidentally broke her gardening equipment because of her enhanced vampiric strength. Freya began to learn more about herself. She had stronger senses and nature. Taste, sound, sight, speed, smell, strength; though she could not eat too much human food otherwise she would get sick. Her weakness to the sun though restricted her life to night-time. Life was lonely. Freya began to adapt to a new lifestyle and learned to live with the fact that she would never see Oliver again. This was one of the reasons she forced herself into this life, she punished herself for pushing her brother away. One day though someone knocked on her door. Freya opened the wooden door.

In the dark, she saw a tall masculine man. He walked up to her, and she could see his face more clearly under the dim-lit candle. It was Hastein. Freya let him in. He sat down on a creaking wooden chair.
Freya asked: 'What are you doing here, Hastein? I thought after Elleswith's death you were too devastated to hang about.'
Hastein said in a husk tone: 'I came here because I decided to look over you and Oliver.'

Freya shook her head and said: 'Forget it, Oliver he-he left.'
Hastein: 'What's wrong with you Freya?'
Freya did not reply.
Hastein: 'Sensitive topic, alright, I understand but know this, I
will not leave. I swore fealty to Elleswith. But she is deceased and
because she cared about you, I now pledge my loyalty to you, Freya
Lothbrok.' Freya grimaced.
Freya: 'Do as you wish but stay out of my way. Oliver turned me
into a vampire, now I have to learn to live like this and maybe ...'
She looked up at the barren ceiling.
She said: 'Maybe have forgiveness.'

Hastein noticed that something had happened between Oliver and
Freya. Something sad. Hastein though did not mind. He stayed at
Freya's side for as long as he had left and taught her the proper way of
farming crops. He helped her repair the nearly run-down farmhouse she
lived in. And so, for a while, there was peace.

Meanwhile, in Kattegat, all the survivors of the aftermath rebuilt
their lives. Everything was back as it was. A new ruler was put onto the
throne of Norway which was appointed by King Harald's son who was
the new regent in Sweden. Peace prevailed for a time. Unprecedented
peace. The Vaeringjar army was disassembled. As if it never had
existed. The advisors of the new king edited the entire records of the
house of Lothbrok. Ivar had died in battle. Sigurd had been killed by
Ivar. Hvitserk disappeared somewhere and never returned. Bjorn died of
fatal wounds. His wife killed herself due to her loss. Aslaug went to
search for her long-lost husband Ragnar and never returned to Kattegat.
Bjorn had two children, Asa and Oliver who never had the chance to
grow up and died as infants. The citizens of Kattegat put the past with
Lothbrok behind them. They wanted to forget the true story of Lothbrok.
Nobody cared. And it was as if all of Freya's deeds and achievements
had been lost in time itself. Nobody remembered her. It said in her
records: That her parents failed to raise her. A good Asa is a dead Asa.
Even the shield maidens forgot her, even though in the time she had
been a shield maiden, she had been one of the most successful to have
ever existed. Just like Lagertha from the Danas period. Indeed, Freya
was now nothing more and nothing less than a legend. Just like
Lagertha. Frode was the only one who struggled to remove Freya from
his memory, he wrote down her story but in order to avoid suspicion, he
wrote it in a strange riddle.

He wrote into a parchment: *You who is not me, forget me and*
leave me hanging in a tree. A gust of wind may blow me away, I

will not stray, but stand and pound my axe to the rhythm of my heart onto my shield. I fought and never lost. My strength was never appreciated because I was chained by secrets and pride. Who am I but a legend lost in time? My question resonates in this song, a tale of woe, is there anyone who cannot also tell me so? I am noble in my name and blood though people only thought of me as an endless tormenting flood. In my time of need, nobody ever heeded me. Alas, I am just a memory that had no meaning. This story is not of a hero nor villain, one must look towards the sky to find my resolution.'

The parchment was written and hidden by Frode in a nook by the statue of Freya back at the temple.

Though in the future, as the Vikings were more and more Christianised, their religion was soon to be destroyed and eradicated bit by bit. Frode did not live to see the temple destroyed. All the ancient texts were either stolen, sold, or hidden. However, what became of the parchment with Freya's riddle?

Many centuries later: in the year 1803, Norway:
Freya had finally adapted more to the sunlight. Strangely, over the centuries, her skin became more and more immune to the sunlight's deadly rays. She was a very old vampire and even discovered that there were more like her out there by talking to others. The connection of demons scattered across the world was called the Hidden Empire, though she refrained herself from trying to discover more of this so-called society. Thanks to Hastein (who had died centuries ago) she was now more experienced and calm-tempered, although Freya still had her issues every now and then. In this day, Freya was in the centre of the village looking for new crops
she could plant when she saw a tall masculine-looking muscle lady.
This toughie woman turned around to Freya and a disgusting stench drafted to Freya. It reeked of garlic. Freya squinted her eyes and covered her nose.
The woman whined: 'What! You have the most rotten manners I've ever witnessed!'
Freya's eyebrows twitched.
She said to the woman: 'You have the most rotten breath I've ever smelt.'
The woman frowned and said: 'Why you have no business insulting my mouth!'
Freya yelled: 'And you have no business insulting me in the first place!'
The woman said: 'Whatever, grumpy pants, my name is Gerta.'

Freya stepped back and said: 'More like grotesque.'

Gerta shouted: 'What! When a woman says she doesn't understand you, she's giving you a second chance to change what you said!'

Freya frowned: 'You are a problem.'

Gerta: 'A smile is going to crack your face missy.'

Freya gritted her teeth and complained: 'Hah, sounds awfully ridiculous coming from you, muscle tank!'

Gerta growled: 'Shut up!'

Freya: 'My name isn't missy, it's Freya!'

Gerta talked loudly: 'How am I supposed to know that Frya, I'm not a psychic. According to you, I'm a muscle tank.'

Freya: 'It's Freya not Frya, I'm not fried.'

Gerta and Freya looked at the infuriated shop keep.

The man said: 'Take your yelling and shouting match elsewhere.'

Freya went to her home, Gerta followed behind. When they were there, Gerta's eyes lit up.

She shouted with joy: 'Potatoes!'

Freya frowned over the masculine woman who swooned over a bunch of crops.

Gerta said: 'You know what, you're okay after all.'

Freya complained: 'Heck, potatoes convinced you of this!'

Gerta said in pride: 'I am tenth in line from my distant relative Hastein, the famed potato farmer of Denmark who served the house of Yanmir. My potato cooking and growing skills go beyond anyone's comprehension.'

Freya burst into a fit of laughter: 'Ha ha ha, I'm sure it does!'

Gerta growled loudly: 'Hey, Vampirella, you are a real meany!'

Freya became serious again and asked: 'What do you mean by Vampirella?'

Gerta: 'Stop the act, I know that you are a vampire.'

Freya asked: 'How?'

Gerta: 'You know, there are other mythical beings other than demons. If you want, I can teach you all of the mythical beings I know.'

Freya asked: 'Are you a Scandinavian water horse?'

Gerta said: 'Yes, so you do have a brain.'

Gerta went inside.

Freya said: 'What do you think you are doing? You can't stay here and live with me!'

Gerta said: 'Well, Frya, you ain't getting rid of me from this potato heaven.'

Freya: 'Oh great, you remind me of your ancestor Hastein.'

Gerta: 'You knew Hastein?'

Freya: 'I lived during his timeframe before I was a vampire, so yes.'

Gerta: 'Well where is he now?'

Freya: 'Buried here somewhere.'

Gerta rejoiced: 'In that case I'm definitely staying here.'

Freya followed Gerta inside and said: 'For the dozenth time its Freya not Frya!'
And so, Gerta moved in with Freya. Gerta cooked every night a mash potato and at breakfast cooked potatoes.

Every night she would say: 'MASH!'

And batched a spoonful or more onto Freya's plate. Freya ate the mushy stuff. It tasted worse than it looked, though Gerta forced Freya to eat the same goop every night. Gerta and Freya became a team. And five years later in 1808, Freya would steal a wallet from a man who later came to work for Gerta and Freya. He stayed for a while and left. He had been called Frances Owen Gregory. Freya found he was a very goofy but reliable person and only became annoyed if one touched his books or suitcase without his knowledge.

Time passed. Gerta aged. Eventually, Freya was forced to leave. She had been in that place way too long. It was a miracle that people hadn't questioned Freya's age for the centuries she had lived there. This was only possible because Freya lived in the shadows and only left the house very little. But now just to be safe, Freya left and entrusted the farm to Gerta. Freya went on a journey to find more of her own kind though she did her own search as she did not want the Hidden Empire knocking on her door. She had heard rumours of demons originating from the middle east. Then later that journey would lead her to a place now known today as America.

Somewhere in a bar in America in the year 2006:
Freya was sitting on a chair in a bar, listening to the public radio. Freya was a vampire from the old age now living in the modern age. Her skin had become so immune to the sunlight that she was now able to become a day-walker. There was a bartender, an African-American woman cleaning out a glass. Freya found the woman's stern nature a bit nerve-racking. Freya noticed the woman's eyes were glued on her every now and then, watching Freya's every move. Freya avoided eye contact. Most of the time. Until she spotted a tattoo on the woman's wrist. Freya had alarm bells ringing in her head. Being a vampire, she automatically recognised the mark of the hunt. The secret clan of Inuit descendants who specialised in hunting mythical beings, mostly vampires. She decided to play a bit with this huntress. Freya casually stood up and went outside the bar. She hid in a corner. The bartender woman came out and looked about. Freya snuck up behind the woman, though the woman turned around and sidestepped. The woman balled her hand into a fist and intended to punch Freya. Freya caught the fist with her hand, twisted the wrist and took her other hand, and punched the

woman in the stomach. The African-American woman fell to her knees. She breathed heavily.

Freya said: 'So, you sensed what I am even though you are only a human.'

The woman grunted. She said: 'You know nothing of me, vampire.'

Freya: 'You let that tattoo on your wrist protrude, I could see it with ease, you are of the hunt.'

The woman said: 'You have a right to know one thing.'

Freya: 'What a buzzkill, you really wasted my time in that bar, I was intending to meet up with someone I hadn't seen in a while.'

The woman said: 'You have the right to know the name of the person that is going to annihilate you.'

Freya said: 'Is that so? You couldn't even knock me over, let alone land a punch.'

The woman sprung up and threw a handful of dirt at Freya. Freya ran away.

The woman said: 'Do not talk so big, vampire, my name is Ontari, if you wish to know your enemy's name.'

Freya showed herself and patted Ontari on the shoulder. Ontari looked behind her, but no one was there.

Freya shouted: 'Hey, over here!'

Ontari looked over to the vampire that stood by her ... motorbike.

Freya said menacingly: 'This your ride, it's very nice.'

Ontari yelled: 'Why you, get away from there!'

Freya got into the vehicle. She waved to Ontari. The motorbike roared to life.

Ontari checked her pockets for the motorbike keys.

She yelled: 'You stole my keys, you bastard!'

Freya: 'Just face it, I'm smarter than you. And by the way, you have the right to know something.'

Ontari growled: 'I know for one, get off now!'

Freya: 'You have the right to know the name of the person that's about to steal your motorbike, it's Freya, Freya Ironside.'

The motorbike skidded away from the area and zoomed off.

Ontari stood there shouting: 'I'll get you, damn vampire, even if it's the last thing I have to do!!'

Freya, who could hear Ontari's yelling from afar on the motorbike, said in her mind: I wish you the best of luck and catch me if you can. A voice that sings never truly disappeared from my mind. It still guides me today. And thanks to it, I can still find my way. In this story of mine, I've experienced loss, devastation, and loneliness. But I am strong. And I will always stand strong even if one sings me a song of the dead.

Revenge of the Hunter

Ontari - The hunter:
Revenge is a dish best served cold

ntari was a black woman from America, but her father came
from Africa and her mother from Canada. It was the year
2004 and Ontari was nineteen years of age. Ontari was born
in the year 1985 and ever since she can remember, her parents told her
all about mythical beings and folklore. Right now, she was in Canada
visiting her grandmother and grandfather. Brad and Ellie Dalketh were
two friendly old people, both in their eighties, and lived on a small farm
with chickens and a dog who was a Canadian Eskimo dog (a Qimmmi)
named Ralfie. On the day she arrived at her grandparent's place, she
went inside the old white coloured house and into Brad and Ellie's
bedroom.
She saw her grandfather lying on his death bed. For many years now,
Brad's heart was failing him and now had given up hope. Ontari looked
at her grandmother (Ellie) who was crying, a face of pure sadness.
Brad in a low pained voice says: 'Ontari, my granddaughter, come sit.'
Ontari sat down on a stool and held his hand. Brad speaks: 'Poor
Ontari, you left us with a heart and mind filled with hatred. It pains
me to speak the truth, but I wish I could have given up all of my
strength to wash away your anger.'
He moaned then spoke again: 'When you first came to us, I ... I saw
those eyes of yours filled with sadness and memories of misery. Back
then, I wanted to ask you, why little girl, must you carry such a burden?'
Ontari shuddered heavily trying not to give in to sadness.
Brad says: 'Every day when I saw you hide away in a corner, I wanted
to tell you it was all going to be alright ... and that you shouldn't blame
yourself for your parents' deaths. And that if you wanted to blame
someone, I would be there to take that burden from you.'
Ontari breathed heavily.
Brad speaks: 'Ellie once told me that she also couldn't stand your
sadness, but she decided with me that in order to not make you feel
worse we locked away our feelings and kept on watching you grow ...
into a never-ending story of sorrow. Now that I think back, I truly
think that I should have held your hand all the way ... alongside Ellie

and maybe you would be able to smile again someday and say goodbye.'

Brad cried out in agony.

Ontari screeched: 'No grandfather, don't go, don't go!'

Brad looked at Ontari and smiled for the last time and said to her:

'Do not weep, for it is my time to be reaped.'

Ontari screamed: 'Noooooo! No No No!'

Then she remembered the dark memory from nine years ago: her parents being torn apart in front of her by vampires.

Ontari was filled with immense sadness and cried over and over again 'til she could cry no more. Then balled her hands into fists, ran outside, and shouted why! Ontari knew now that her grandfather was not killed by accident, but by a reaper and Brad knew that, for Ellie told Ontari later on, that Ralfie had been barking at something in Brad's room the day before Ontari's visit. Ontari was angry and she wanted vengeance, for Brad and her parents. Nobody would stop her 'til she got want she wanted.

Word Glossary

Book of Light:
A special ancient book that has been rumoured to have been around for a long time, hidden in human civilisations, even the most ancient ones. It is a book of prophecies that foretell things to come and that it was written by the Ancients; the Ancients were the god like creatures created by the all mother according to Elleswith's recount in Sing me a song of the dead. Over the centuries the book of light has been rumoured to have disappeared according to mythical creature beliefs but nobody knows where.

The Hidden Empire:
Is the name of the demon empire/society. Mostly is known as a secret society of demons scattered across the world. Their secret world that they can go to is the underworld. All demons accord to the rules of this empire and they are governed by the Demon King Lucien as well as the King's council.

Tyrfing:
Is rumoured to be a sword from the gods (the Ancients). Can destroy armies or call upon the dead as well as that it cannot be destroyed in any way. According to stories about the last wielder, she was seen channelling magic using the blade but this is only possible if a magic stone is added to the sword. One story of the witches is that it was hidden in the black sea by the last wielder and that its where it still is; others say nobody knows the true location of the relic. Another relic similar to the Tyrfing sword is the sword from the Lorelei family, it is said to have the same or similar powers to the Tyrfing sword and it can enhance powers for anyone who has Lorelei blood in their veins; also shield a Lorelei descendant from harm.

World Hunt Organisation:
Mostly referred to as the WHO organisation. An organisation situated in America that specialises in training humans to kill bad or disorderly mythical creatures. Their leader is always a woman and is called 'the Oracle'.

Would our other books be of interest?

Seeing Beings is Believing Chronicles — A Dynasty of Cat People Part — Book 1 — e & K. Kim

Seeing Beings is Believing Chronicles — Sing Me a Song of the Dead — Book 2 — e & K. Kim

Seeing Beings is Believing Chronicles — The Legend of the Dullahan — Book 3 — e & K. Kim

Order of the Grim Reaper Origins — Seeing Beings is Believing Chronicles — Book 4 — e & K. Kim

Born to Bjorn Ironside and the former slave-turned-shield-maiden Þorunn, Freya Ironside was heir to greatness - but scorned by her father and left to be raised by her grandmother Aslaug. Trained by her legendary uncles, Freya rose as a fierce shield maiden and later as a priestess devoted to the Old Norse ways.

Her fate takes a strange turn when she meets Elleswith, an elven creature. When Freya is gravely wounded in battle, her brother turns her into a vampire to save her life - a decision she never forgives.

Now, part warrior, part immortal, Freya wanders the northern wilds, crossing paths with the Hidden Empire - a secret demon realm ruled by a dark king. From blood-soaked battlefields to quiet moments in time. Freya's tale is one of legend, rage, and transformation. A saga of action, magic, love, and vengeance - this is the journey of a woman forged in myth, caught between worlds.

'Seeing Beings' is indeed the path to 'Believing'.

www.ingramcontent.com/pod-product-compliance
Lightning Source LLC
Chambersburg PA
CBHW071145250626
47159CB00006B/2298